C000263847

Femke

DAVID CAMERON

TAPROOT PRESS

First published by Taproot Press 2023

ISBN: 978-1838080082

The author's right to be identified as author of this book under the Copyright, Designs and Patents Act 1988 has been asserted.

Printed and bound by
Replika Press, India

Typeset in 12 point Garamond by
Main Point Books, Edinburgh

Cover design: Stephen Cameron
Cover drawing (woman's head): Wilson Russell

To whom else?

PART ONE

The Careless Acrobat

Mother often had premonitions she'd speak about afterwards. I can't square the Mother I knew as a young kid with the suburban Mama of now. Back then she was a witch. Father, I think, thought so – I could see he was in awe of her. She was something of a singer in those days. Strictly small-time operettas. I got a telling-off once when I tried her home-made cold medicine, though the taste was punishment enough. She was capable of drinking during the day. Once father was gone, I had visions of us losing everything.

My weirdness I blamed on her. This was in the time of tests. I remember sills and sills of spider plants in a long corridor with mad paintings along it. The first time Mother really hit me was to get me out of a trance. Then it became punishment for going into one.

Her job was to have old friends round and do their hair for them. I expect there was too much time spent alone, alone or with me – the way she stared through me, it was almost the same thing. At least I had dead hair to play with.

I'd watch Mother fill up with emptiness between phone calls, in the hours waiting for Father to come. I liked those mornings when she was on the phone and sounding animated, I didn't care how much, I never feared her manic side. I knew I was in for a good day then. What scared me was her monotone. (I shivered just then, thinking about it, and I was already shivering.)

She was suspicious of me. I fed her suspicions without wanting to. She had suspected Father. There were odd words, tears, famously a plate smeared with ketchup thrown against a wall (blood, I told my friends), which I understood suddenly: Father was having an affair. I doubt this now. He did have a glamorous secretary, possibly more than one. I only ever saw the one. My sole time in Daddy's office. There was a man called Clark or Clerk – Clark Kent was a name I knew – who stood the whole time Father sat: I remember Father's voice being harsher than in the house. Africa was mentioned. I'd been given a toy snake with brown and beige scales and was playing with it. The secretary appeared as she was about to leave. She was wearing white gloves.

Talking about Father's death won't warm me up. One thing, though: it made us richer. Now that the money's gone – or, more likely, tied up in something – I'm glad. It's cleaner that way.

I learned all about men once Father was dead. A beautiful widow with a pubescent girl isn't nothing. They came sniffing round, pawed us a little, ran off, then they'd come sniffing back. (Why do I lie? We were safe enough in our house. Only the insurance man – Mother had a lot of dealings with him – got further than the doorstep.) Mother's body had thickened before grief went to work on it. In the photo I have of the two of us from then, taken by some monkey making a display before Mother, she is alarmingly beautiful.

Holidays were worst. One man I remember: Mother called him Shoe Shuffle Man. We had just stepped off the boat when mechanically the music started up – twenty minutes it played for – and Mother did three or four steps of a dance with me. Always the same steps, danced from girlhood on, maybe to this day. Shoe Shuffle Man appears, sliding his moccasins across the planks, arms raised in a 'May I?' gesture, but directed towards me in order to get to Mother, who was now walking smartly into the reception area. A smoker's laugh and a few words of song, which Mother foolishly turned and smiled back at. He dogged us the whole holiday then. There was only the promenade, so it was easy for him. His grey-blue slacks were perfectly pressed. Why does that generation of men hate women? Mother despised them. She felt she shouldn't, but she did. Father at least had something gutsy about him, looked almost like Robert Mitchum at times. (I loved watching old movies, curled up on the sofa.) He must have seemed an odd fish to those slacked shufflers. Those Clarks or Clerks.

Another time, now. Not a holiday snap, this one – Father was even alive. I was singing in the choir. I'd coaxed Mother to come along and she was quite taken with us, spoke respectfully to our prim teacher. The girl behind me sang with a hissing sweetness that drove me to belt out the hymns. Only the mothers stayed behind, and one father it looked like, until everyone was accounted for. No, he was simply 'a music lover', he said. You couldn't even accuse him of being a lover of small girls. I was put into my coat by him. He had charmed Mother enough to have us waiting by the kerb while he fetched his car. I think I expected a Mercedes-Benz, but it wasn't that. The ugliest thing was the plastic covering on the seats. I asked about it, was told not to. I asked again, as if I hadn't heard, as if that girl was still hissing in my ear. It came out that his wife was liable to roll around and dribble. Something incurable. Mother coughed and his neck grew red, while I squeaked on the plastic.

Bibi has what I need. I walk him all hours in this druggy park. We go round the lake and he sniffs the ducks – they have no fear here. Nobody has any fear.

I send him into the bushes and he brings back the stick and I send him in again, and then the men come out, the young one first, the hustler, who if he recognises me always laughs. Bibi knows these boys too. I'd pass the time of day with them, but they have nothing to say. Little at first, and later, nothing.

I think I've exhausted this park, then something new turns up. I found out a girl was discovered in leaf mould the year I was born. That was near the hyacinths. There was a service, hyacinths were planted. If there was a plaque on some tree or bench, it's been ripped out. That was the right thing to do: parks are for the living.

I know where to go on nights like this. Not the streets tourists flock to before the weather turns. One street in particular I like: New Mirror Street. There are some poor there – they have a deal going that means they never leave. Only the rich sometimes move out, and what they don't want, I take. I'm not the only one, God knows. But if stuff's in my hands, sweetheart, try taking it from me. (I talk like this sometimes. Don't be put off. When I bark, Bibi barks, and that soothes me. Then I can hold my breath for five minutes at a time.)

I met my ex in this park. I saw all this as a kid, was wheeled through the gates out of the park, looked up at the same old clock on the burnt church. Now it's mainly offices. I don't mind, I hated that gloomy church. Though old people could doze in it when the park was freezing. The gates are the same too. Wonderful wrought iron, with a design you think is dragons but is only plant stems. Now the man who made those gates, I'd like to speak to him for a day. Just listen and nod sometimes and let him ask me about Bibi and anything he wanted really. I wouldn't mind sitting beside a man like that.

I'm not in the mood for the market today. All that fowl hanging upside down and making Bibi excited. I'd sooner take my chances in the museum. When you're hungry, you can cope with the smell of must better than roasting chicken. It's my own fault, I shouldn't walk so much. Walking is always fatal. Each day I tell myself I'll stay still tomorrow. Tomorrow comes and I'm halfway round the city before I remember. Why should I complain? Bibi doesn't. I see hunger in his eyes sometimes, and I love him so much for trying to hide it.

'Cappuccino, with nutmeg,' I tell the boy in the coffee cart. Whenever I feel poor I spend money. This won't be much, and I avoid looking down at Bibi. There's nothing for you here, boy, anyway.

I'm talking to my dog.

I am called Femke. People think it a beautiful name. I've no opinion. That's who I am and I have to live with it. I'm not suggesting anyone call their daughter Femke. I think it's older people who like it best – maybe there were more Femkes in their day.

It hasn't given me a beautiful nature. I've had a habit since I was twelve of tilting back my head and rolling my eyes till the whites show – tests revealed I 'elect to do it', which makes me hateful. I don't have visions or say anything memorable, though I do moan – 'eerily', I am told.

Mother used to call me twisted. There's a Chinese proverb: cut a blade of grass and you shake the universe. When I heard that, from the ex I met in the park – it was our first meeting – I tore handfuls and handfuls of grass in a frenzy.

It's nothing but a big barn where I live. There'll be people there when it's offices: the work keeps getting put back. I've lived in a place like it before, also near the harbour. I'd sneak old friends in and out, till everyone got too casual and I couldn't shift them even on days when the owner came round. I don't make the same mistake twice. It's not as if I have to explain myself. My name was mud in the squats long ago.

The owner comes round here too. I almost look forward to it. He's got a bronzed complexion – maybe has a timeshare in a hot climate – and a man-in-his-mid-40s' paunch. Still thinks he can run it off.

He made a move on me once while showing me the gas heater. It came as a surprise. I hadn't been shown how to use one before and was quite interested – if I could be anything I'd be an electrician or engineer. We were both hunkered, but his knees had cracked a second or so before he put a hand on my knee. 'I think not,' was what I said. (Quite proud of that 'I think not'.) He said it had just been to balance himself. I didn't laugh. Now he mews round the place for half an hour then leaves.

There are advantages to being pretty. You know that the men who are nasty to you are psychopaths. Today you'd do well to make out my looks – I could care if there was a point. I don't want to be drawing too many glances in these streets. Men can be cruel, but when I look hard at them and they see me better, they change their tune. Except the psychos. Bibi is handy for them. He's part-Alsatian. I wouldn't say he spots them a mile off, but he knows when I'm distressed.

I did get entangled with one psycho. It hurts me to say it, but he looked a lot like Van Gogh. I have an affection for that bearded misfit, and not just because I'm fond of foxgloves and fields of wheat. The psycho was in tweeds but practically homeless. I spent a month in his company.

He had a passion for identifying bodies. Told the police his sister was missing and could he check any stiffs they had. I laughed at this, because it's funny. Less funny when the man is next to you drooling over the word 'suppurating'. We would walk along and look into houses, and he would really fume at all the softness we saw. Well, I've felt that way too, but I was nostalgic for it at the same time. I told him so. He threw me down and tried to break my head on a bollard.

I wish I could feel the cold less. I would seriously like my puppy fat back. I last had it living with Mother in the sort of suburban existence that's the same the world over. So I imagine. Even when we lived in the city we had a summerhouse. It was in one of those depressing beehives of summerhouses on the outskirts, where nobody gets buried in leaf mould, and the dragonflies are the size of your hand. I found it impossible to feel haunted there. Couldn't even throw my head back.

Father died on my twelfth birthday.

There's this one place I eat where the waitress exposes an inch or two of her middle and it's just a seam of fat. She's not bad-looking, she just has that seam of fat. I'd love to roll it between my fingers. People can't tell with my jumper and parka how thin I can be. Because it does vary. Six months ago if I'd spun like a coin I'd have vanished.

The boy in the park's name was Herman. His flat was in the street I passed ten minutes ago wrapped up in thoughts of Mother. Bibi normally strains at the leash, and might have done this time too. Herman left the city and me for good two years ago. Three years ago now.

He would feed Bibi a dog biscuit, one end in his own mouth. He clowned about like that when I wanted him to be serious, was serious when I wanted him to be funny. It got on my nerves. He was always making some point or other, *educating* me I suppose. I didn't like to be educated.

Herman is the type of man women love *as a friend*. I don't have time for that sort of thing, and I *know* he was grateful. He wasn't the clumsy lover you'd expect either.

My trances – he was the first to call them that – only amused him. They tended to happen in his room. He would crush the tablets in his inhaler into a powder and breathe that in, thinking he could join me this way. I know it's funny. It's funny, but I don't understand it. I felt safe in his room. I don't know why the trances came.

He was spoiled by the fact he had a sister he was too close to. I'm judging by the stories he told, and what I made out myself, but I never met her. He said they could be nostalgic even for the moment that was passing. I see her as a skinny puppet bobbing about with Herman her puppet-brother. They're both saying, '*This* moment, no *this* moment, no *this...*'

We ended as we began, with a walk through the park. I

avoided the place for a while, swallowed my pride, and stayed with some old squatter friends, telling them I had to 'sort my head out', which is the kind of language they still understand.

There is a flaky blue sill underneath the huge window at the front and that's my garden. I have an assortment of roots and stems in makeshift pots there, sticking up at the sky. Perhaps in summer it will all be conventionally beautiful. It is beautiful now. I fill two bottles with water at the garage. In summer I can make two or three trips and have enough for whatever's sprouting on the sill. There are always things to look forward to. By summer I'll have been thrown out, no doubt, with one more grope for good luck.

You'd need this metal door to feel safe. The water comes past here, and you wouldn't believe the noise water makes unless you've lived next to it. There's plenty of iron and wood for it to slap against. I've fallen asleep with my hands over Bibi's ears. Sometimes I see faces at the window. You can buy white linen from the market for next to nothing: one day I'll get a roll of it and block them out.

I had an attic room before, crammed full, now it's as if it's all been stretched like a balloon. I keep what I need in one corner, what I don't need everywhere else. I've a Ghana goddess to keep me fertile: it's the real thing. We get in when the world's going out normally, I cook something on the gas stove, wash up and play with Bibi, and next thing there are no lights on in the suburbs. There's a view of them at the far end. By one, maybe two, they're a sheet of black.

I can lie flat and look at nothing then. I'm the opposite in the morning. That's one thing that's changed about me over the years. I get up when I wake up, am up with the fishermen, in fact. Bibi would lie longer, I'm sure. Poor dog, it's like every day he gets more human.

At least in the past he had a garden not concreted over where he could soak up the sun and not have me tugging him endlessly here and there. One thing I don't miss from that garden is the awful sundial (Mother's idea). I have one luminous blue-green alarm clock turned to the wall, which I look at when I must. I made the owner make appointments and it helps me see that he keeps them. Otherwise it could go.

Covering mirrors is another thing I do. Not with sheets, just some jumpers and towels. They're my mirrors, picked up on the street. I look at myself in them when the notion comes over me, then cover them again. Tonight something's made me anxious, I don't know what. I'm not going to do anything different or go outside again. I'll just lie down beside Bibi and see if he stirs. Not blow the candles out.

Seems like everything is beginning again. I've opened the windows, let the wind play havoc with anything light. Bibi is retrieving one thing after another, barking his head off, and – I swear it – smiling that wolf-smile of his. I think I'll get the death mask of Beethoven I saw in the east. Bibi can furrow his brows too when he wants.

Everything *is* beginning – has already begun… They were dancing underneath the clock in the square, regimented couples, out in the February morning cold – I only stopped to laugh. I got swept up in it in no time. Of course the junkies were there, swinging and stumbling, and grinning to an audience they thought appreciated them. The old dears, on the other hand, were stony-faced but in their element. People my age were sniggering, and a few cowards shouted out. Then he stepped forward. Slipped between two barriers. A woman was left stranded when her partner had a coughing fit, but before she could affect concern for him, a much younger man appeared. Only for a few seconds, it seemed, then the waltz was over. If the loudspeakers hadn't abruptly blared out a new tune, my eyes might have strayed again. He drew himself up like a bullfighter. What followed caught everyone's eye: the most beautifully danced tango, from an odd couple decades apart in age. I started off the applause at the end.

And that was it. He said a few words to the beaming woman and slipped back into the crowd. Next thing he was walking briskly, travelling bag in hand, to the side of the palace near the Old Church.

He was the dancing harlequin on my old music-box at home. I liked it that a man so young had taken the trouble to learn those steps. Lying in bed, I tried to picture what his life was like. He'd learnt the steps so well, but he didn't seem stuffy or old-fashioned. I could see a sister or a young mother – not in a Herman way. No, this woman was coolly detached.

I found that I couldn't picture his life after all, that what I'd been dreaming of was the life I might have had with him.

The next time I saw him was even briefer. I was in a number fourteen tram and he was at a traffic island, one hand behind him on the bike holding his bag. The same bag. Any impulse to get up and go to him would have been smothered by so many bodies anyway. I could have rapped on the window with my ring (Herman's). I'm too self-contained. I'd seen him twice now in the space of, I don't know, ten days. I might see him again.

I increased the chances of it by walking Bibi where his bike had pointed, in both directions. If this seems obsessive, I admit I can be that. But I don't think so. It was sort of a game I could lose or win and it wouldn't matter. The old roads had gone a bit stale. There was even some interesting stuff put out there.

The third sighting sealed it. Mrs Bijl, the widow who lets flats out, was at the canal feeding her birds – I think every bird in the city. She turned before I could call out, walked to where someone was knocking on an open door. I was paralysed. Bibi sniffed at the weeds in the cracks, wondering what I saw in them.

He turned towards me, then half-turned to where he'd been. It let me look at him. I would have kept on looking, but there was Mrs Bijl's hand, bleeding into a polythene bag filled with mouldy bread. One of the birds, presumably. She spoke while rolling the bread between her fingers.

'Nothing less than a thousand, otherwise the council can poke its nose in. How does that sound?'

Now I was on the steps too, one hand on the frosty railing, acting like I was second in line.

'What do *you* want?' she said to me, then to him: 'You're not with her?'

'Alas, no,' he said, not meaning it. So he was English.

She fixed her eyes on me again. 'Come with my money?'

I drew Bibi close, knowing she'd soften at the sight of him. It was what got me a place before.

With the bargaining in full swing, Mrs Bijl tried using his first name for leverage. She didn't have to prise it out of him: Alistair. He was so insincere I couldn't be sure. He spelled it out slowly for us.

Mrs Bijl said she had the perfect place for him, nothing for me. I'd played it safe, said five hundred was my limit. I still hadn't spoken to him when she dissolved into the hallway. What I said now would have to count. Finally I found some inspiration.

'Hello, dancer.'

'You mean my tango in the square?'

'That's right,' I said, pleased that he understood me straight away. His astonished look turned into a grin.

'I'd just landed an hour before. You weren't dancing too, were you?'

'I was taking my dog Bibi for a walk. I only stopped to laugh.'

'Oh, you were one of them.'

I felt foolish explaining that I wasn't *one of them* while he said hello to Bibi and stroked him and didn't ask my name.

Mrs Bijl came back in a green coat that looked like it was made out of *rope*, old rope dyed green. It seemed to take her an age to close the door. All I could see was the coat. Brown buttons, as prominent as her knuckles, buttonholes like eyes or like knots in wood, old wood. She was panting like an engine inside that coat.

He warmed to me a little now, I thought. We didn't know where we were headed, but with Mrs Bijl's health, it couldn't be far. He had told her he wanted the dog there when he checked out the flat, that an animal was a good judge. He winked at me after he said it.

The old widow had a gift for finding cheaper places in good streets, basement or attic flats normally.

I saw he didn't have his bag today.

'Are you staying at a hostel?'

'At a hotel,' he said. 'An interesting one. Deserted most of the time, but the man who runs it has a withered arm. I like watching him cope at mealtimes.'

He said odd things like that and then was silent. I was beginning to get a sense of him already. He had long legs but I managed to keep step with him. (We stopped to let Mrs Bijl catch up, or when we didn't know where to go.) There was something dark in his complexion, Arabic or Hispanic, I couldn't be sure.

'Where do you come from?' I asked at one more crossroads. Bibi was pulling on the lead, anxious to be petted by Mrs Bijl.

'London,' he said. 'You're from here, right? I thought so. The women have a certain look, squareish in the jaw, almost masculine. It's not so pronounced in you. Don't be offended, my mother was Dutch.'

'I'm not offended,' I said, truthfully. 'I like honesty. Tell me about your mother.'

'Are you a gardener?' he asked next, ignoring my question. 'I noticed you've gardening fingers.'

I was offended now, and put my hands away. He didn't seem to care about embarrassment. I told him about my place not having water.

'Sounds like a good place,' he said when I'd described it fully to him. 'I'd like to see it some day. What's your name?'

He told me I was free to visit him any time at the place we were going to see. 'I'm too intrigued by this old bag to let it go. And I'm impressed by how nicely she treats waifs and strays like you two.'

The overstretched cable about to snap in my chest relaxed suddenly. I thought the English were super-polite, but this man wasn't. I'd never liked politeness.

Mrs Bijl had stopped for more than breath and was waving us back. 'She's straight out of a 40s British spy film,' Alistair said. 'The charlady busy badmouthing the milkman while evil's hatching out all around her. Meant to be the salt of the earth.'

Now she was in front, taking us down a lane lined with bushes, so that the canal was screened fom view.

I didn't know the place. It soon opened onto a rectangle of tarmac. She stopped us, an arm raised wearily, pointing to a window. 'Entrance other side,' was all she managed to say.

Alistair put an arm through hers and spoke in that rumblingly deep voice that reassures old people.

The carpeted, narrow stairs in the stairwell led to a door painted the kind of blue-green you see in hospitals. There was a biscuity smell inside, a toilet bowl Mrs Bijl tried to screen from us, then a room with dark furniture, another room with a humped-up bed in it, and a small kitchen. Alistair spent a lot of time at the mantelpiece, Mrs Bijl in an armchair, coat loosened despite the cold, while I inspected the place. Bibi sniffed the bed. I walked back into the living room and waited for Alistair to speak. I was feeling uneasy again. I couldn't have said why.

Alistair, the back of his head huge in the rope-held mirror, was turned to face us. He said: 'Somebody died here, Mrs Bijl.'

3

Almond eyes. They're the words I can't get out of my head. The word. Almond-eyed. Almondeyed.

I've seen him naked, so I know his body too. He doesn't care who sees him undress. He offered me the chance of a shower, but I said no, I was a bit prissy about it. This was on the Thursday. The three of us – four of us, remembering Bibi – left last Wednesday after he paid money for the key. He slipped me the key and said to double back, that he'd call round later. He had his bag to fetch. I trust him completely, without believing everything he says.

He's in good shape, not an athlete – there are tiny ripples of fat under his skin, though he looks lean in clothes. He dresses well. I think now I've seen all the clothes he has with him. The shirt hanging in his wardrobe today is my favourite. An odd choice for me since it's brown. Earth-brown. He put it on once and took it off when I said I liked it. It's how he is.

He was right about a person having died. Mrs Bijl looked uncomfortable. I thought she was sizing up the possibility of lying. Alistair is hard to lie to. She glanced up at the light shade, made some chewing movements, and told us about her two ladies. Sisters. The younger died and the elder went into a home, frantic and out of her mind the last time Mrs Bijl had seen her. She'd had a hard job getting the blood out of the carpet. She thought she'd said too much, but Alistair wanted to hear more.

He didn't arrive with his bag till after dark. I hadn't a light on, just the gas fire, which I lay with my face towards, watching my eyes in the metal panels. My skin was dry and my eyes hurt.

He called out my name and I responded with a kind of animal groan. He put the light on in the room, turned it off, went to the kitchen and put the light on there. I could smell the Chinese food he was carrying.

He was singing in a low voice in the kitchen. I rolled to my feet then, tried to walk silently closer, but he heard.

'I bought chopsticks for us to eat with. I don't suppose Tweedledee and Tweedledum had chopsticks in the house. You look red.'

'The fire.'

'You've made me yawn now,' he said, spooning out the last of the food. I'd only yawned to cover up my awkwardness. 'Take these to the table and I'll look for a lamp. Old ladies love lamps.'

We ate in a smell of heated dust, Alistair obsessing about the women, Mrs Bijl too, impersonating her with his English accent. Herman used to say there was a reason for everything, which I believe now, but Alistair would go quiet for a long time for no reason I could see. I thought I understood when he said his own sister was dead. It could explain the interest in the flat and the women. I said as much.

'You're wrong there, my dear,' he said. 'I told you I'd take it before I knew anything about the place. Did you forget?'

After the meal he took out three framed photographs, moving them along the mantelpiece. He put a hand to his mouth and his face looked pale. I guessed that the girl whose picture he was holding was the dead one. She was thirteen, if that.

I pointed to another photo that looked more recent.

'Who's that one, your wife?'

I'd spoken almost without thinking, meaning it as a joke.

'Astute of you,' he said.

'What am I doing here?' I said, my whole skin crawling. I looked round as if I'd possessions to gather up. He handed me Bibi's leash.

'Go if you like. You realise you've not asked a single question about me.'

I snorted at this, but when he said, 'I want you to stay,' I felt disarmed. I very much wanted to stay.

'I meant what I said, that you can come here when you like. We won't be sleeping together. I don't know if that reassures you or disappoints. The day you saw me dancing with that ridiculous woman – I saw you. You were pressed against the fence. I knew we'd meet.'

I stayed the night and made breakfast for us in the morning. We'd both slept on the floor, in different rooms. He didn't trust Mrs Bijl to have washed the bedclothes and I couldn't vouch for her. The many blankets weren't exactly spring-fresh. Bibi slept under some of them too, happy after his meal of rinsed chicken. In the morning I was up early feeling restless, not knowing if I should go. I heard my name called out in a muffled voice, which startled me, till I remembered where I was. Where he was. He told me to take money from his trouser pockets if I wanted anything. I took about half of what there was and got a shopping, a sensible one. I wanted to thank him, and I don't know many ways.

I was feeling light-hearted. I still couldn't bring myself to ask the questions I wanted answered. In daylight only the present moment seems real. We cleaned the place and talked and listened to the radio, a small transistor, not the big old-fashioned wooden affair you'd expect. Bibi was bemused that I wasn't walking him to death. He went uncomplaining with Alistair to somewhere grassy nearby. Ten minutes I'd say they were away. He's a good dog.

I tuned the radio in to a chat show station and eventually Alistair asked what was being said. I lied outrageously.

'You've been wiping that patch of wall for a long time now,' he said.

'I have?'

He walked round me and then wheeled the footstool I was standing on back from the wall. I thought for a second he was going to take my face in his hands like a doctor. I even widened my eyes for him.

'You should take a rest now,' he said. 'I don't think you slept too well last night.'

'I slept fine.'

'I heard whimpering when I woke up.'

'That would be Bibi.'

'It didn't sound like a dog.'

'He gets more human every day.'

He lifted me off the footstool and put me on the sofa, with Bibi barking round us. It was the only time we'd touched. He was a bit breathless and started undressing, calling behind him that I could shower too, after him, if I wanted. I got to my feet to say no and saw the white streak of his flesh in the mirror. He laughed, or perhaps gasped at the floor's coldness.

He was an age in the shower and I started to think about my place again. I didn't like leaving it to get damp. Alistair had wanted to go, but since that conversation he'd said nothing more. It would be better if I got there first. I couldn't decide yet how much of me I wanted him to know. He was right: I hadn't asked him anything. I was burning to, but I didn't want the curiosity returned. I never tell my story to anyone. I mean, I've never spoken enough about myself to anyone for there even to be a story, one that was clear to me. Oh I make up stories about myself in my head all the time. I'm making up this one, after all. It doesn't mean it's not true.

I thought how it would be good now to go and have him wondering about me, then more practically I thought of leaving him a note describing where I lived. He might feel he'd gone too far stripping off. Every plan fell through because I couldn't calculate how he'd react. What I couldn't visualise was him weeping and tearing his hair out. He'd wait till we next met, say something to outdo my 'Hello, dancer' to him, I couldn't think what. Or he would be gone. He could be gone while I walked the streets thinking I haunted him.

4

The boxes have arrived. They're why I've waited inside all day – Alistair had people to see. 'Boxes' was his word. They are crates that came in through the window. Marked *FRAGILE*, except for one – books, judging by the weight. Not that I lifted it, but I watched the men struggling. I've been acting like a cat around new furniture since they arrived. The wood of the crates looks very odd in this old place. There's a smell of newness from them. I wonder if his wife packed them: perhaps her scent is mixed in with the wood's. I think, though, she's a lazy woman. I'll get a chance to prove it if she really does come over. Next month, he thinks – he's already looking for somewhere bigger. I'm not helping. In the space of a week I've grown attached to these dead rooms.

The bedroom is a bit bare. Here there is at least the decoration of Alistair's photographs. I pick them up from time to time, not his wife's. A hidden camera would reveal how often I glance at that one. Which leaves his dead sister. And, behind, his parents. He says they weren't married then, but I can't be sure. I can't see a ring – his mother is wearing white gloves.

He works in film. Is that right? I don't know how to say it. It's as well I don't sleepwalk, with his cameras and equipment spread out over the floor. The video stuff is a bit gaudy, brilliant silver like a new hubcap. There actually weren't any books. I can't wait to see something by him, I know it would be good. He's teaching film at the Academy and will be shooting scenes of his own soon, once his wife is here. I don't see why he has to wait.

'Susan and I had an interesting phone-call yesterday,' he said. 'About you. She suggested something. I wasn't going to say this yet.'

'You spoke to her about *me*?'

'I often speak about you. She thinks I should base my next film on you. She loves the name Bibi. For *you*. I'm in two minds.'

'She sees me as a dog?'

He laughed at this. 'I was about to say you've got the wrong end of the stick. Better not. What do you think of the film idea?'

'I feel like saying no,' I said.

'Then say no. I'll get some lousy student to do it.'

A week ago he would have followed me into the toilet to soothe me. I stood listening with the door unlocked. When I went back to him, he said: 'I'd like to see your squat.'

'It's an anti-squat,' I said, soothing myself by getting the better of him.

'I was thinking of shooting there. We could go tonight.'

I'd gone back in dreams and each time it was further down, a bit more under the earth, the steps spiralling more till I got there. Recently it had been a room of skeletons. I used to like old bones, sheep's jawbones that I picked up in the fields. Not these bones. I recognised dead relations like my aunt. Oh Christ, not grinning. I'm not a psychopath.

He said he'd come later and to give him the address. I had to get there before him, there were things I might not want him to see. I cycled along the canal next to the summerhouses, feeling like a hermit, with all the lovers out in droves.

I put off thinking. It was like being in a groove of memory taking that route again. Like the walk to school you never forget. The different cow-parsley was a wallpaper pattern from my childhood, that sort of feeling. I took a risk and closed my eyes. I was past the summerhouses.

The water was dead still and filmy, and the only sounds were from the all-night factory. A big ship was moored at the end of the street. I worried that this meant more people had been passing my place. I could hardly bear to look.

The hollow stems were still thrusting up in the garden. It was a good sign, I felt. I took the big fairytale key out of my pocket. The door was impossible, but eventually it grated open. The stench inside made me think an animal had crawled in to rot.

I walked round like I was examining a crime scene. I get that guilt from Mother, but once I'm aware of it I can usually shake it off. Suddenly some sunlight broke into the room, moving over a green jumper I'd left on a chair. I lifted the jumper, smelled it – smelled myself in it.

My last morning here was laid out in front of me. It was as if I'd known. Even Bibi's bowl was clean. Apart from a couple of days' washing balled up in a towel, there was nothing I would need to move.

I walked to the white steps which take you to another level, a large alcove too damp to store anything in. I didn't see the water at first, and then I felt it, seeping through my shoes, a half-inch or so, deeper further from the step, like in a swimming pool. It felt right, strangely, like my absence *should* have let water in. It was all there was to mark it.

The alcove with its steps was so pristinely white, even the water didn't make me want to leave immediately. But I did leave, hopping back out of it, taking off a shoe and a sock at a time, not caring where I flung them. I messed up the bed too. It wasn't really a bed.

Alistair made me wait another hour while I sat and deteriorated, thinking about too many things at once. Then I went out like a light, must have. Next to my cheek on the pillow was a pool of drool. It could have been two hours.

I heard a clatter against the metal door and knew it was him. I hadn't locked it, but I had to get up and open it anyway, because he was drunk. A young man was with him – one of his students, presumably. There were no introductions other than first names. The student (I'm sure he was) was wild-looking in that harmless way of students. He staggered from one spot to another being cheerful. Alistair, sobering up, inspected the place coolly.

The student, who was English too, made fun of my name, calling me Kiki and then Famine. Alistair smiled broadly in approval when his inspection was done. He did pick up a sock and say 'naughty', which I smiled at. It got a bit galling, though, being treated like a child, especially by the student who was maybe my age.

'Watch this,' the student said, and proceeded to rip pages out of a notebook.

Now, the notebook was empty, apart from some scribbles – I never could write, I mean write well, and the last time I tried, it was like my hand had forgotten how – but this was too much. I flashed a look at Alistair that told him so.

'You might want to stop that,' he said to him.

'No, no, watch.'

Now the student was bent over the alcove water, steering two paper boats on it with a finger.

'Origami,' he said proudly.

Alistair's mobile rang. I held it to his ear till he could hold it. His composure wasn't quite ice-cool. Keeping my distance, I approached the student with a smile, but with my ears pricked up. Alistair's talk was monosyllabic, slurred. *She* was saying more.

She certainly sounded animated. Her tinny voice was all I could hear, though the student was mouthing words like a goldfish. I brought him a glass of water. Stale water.

'Femke,' Alistair shouted. 'Susan wants a word.'

I swore in panic as he held out the phone. I couldn't believe I was walking towards it.

5

'The Careless Acrobat,' he says. His idea of a title. I think not. Susan agrees with me. She agrees with me, taking up the whole bed in the process. She likes to lie like this, on top of the eiderdown, drink in hand. Port and lemon, an English drink. I know it's only for a week and then the place will be mine. Technically, I'll be back under Mrs Bijl's wing, but with Alistair paying. I don't know for how long. Until they get bored with me.

She is a long skinny woman, dark, dresses well for her age. I first saw her bending over the sink in the kitchen in a cream dress with a grey pattern of roses. She was scrubbing hard at something, something was stained, she turned round with a wild-eyed look and with sweat on her face. Odd to have seen her like that. She quickly melted, if that's the word, softened, like she was recognising me. Not hard to work out who I was, I suppose, I'd let myself in. She wasn't alone. Alistair called her name from the bedroom. My eyes met hers and we sort of laughed. I didn't mean to say her name to her. I think it was the echo of Alistair saying it, going round in my head and escaping again. Susan. Susan. You can say it without really meaning to.

In truth there had been a warm tone to her voice on the phone that time as she asked – calling from the bathtub, I imagined later – 'Is it really you?' It really was me, but how to say so? I'd stolen this woman's husband. She didn't wait for the reply, but said: 'Be a dear and walk away from Alistair so I can speak to you.' I walked until he stopped following me, right into the alcove.

She asked how I was and did I feel put upon by Alistair.

'Put upon?'

'Alistair has a penchant for picking up …'

'Strays?'

'Don't say that. Strong young women like yourself. Remember I know Alistair.'

After a silence she asked what he was doing now. There was something so loving in this question, and I happened to be watching him at the time, that I forgot my anger. He was rearranging my old cuttings of honesty in a tumbler.

Alistair took the phone from me, whispering some words to her, protective of us both, like Father carrying me up to bed on one of Mother's bad days. I whispered to him. Asked him to show his dead-loss friend the door.

Once we were alone, Alistair wanted to know in detail what Susan had said. I said nothing, to tease him and perhaps also because I'm not good at remembering. I have to *wring* the past out of me sometimes.

'We should have come here before,' he said. 'I like it. I like the whiteness. What's this?'

'My Ghana goddess. You can have it if you like. My gift to you. I'm sleepy.' I lay back on the mattress while he squatted next to my middle. 'Lie down,' I said, 'I'm cold.'

It was the first time he'd ever done what I'd asked. We lay fully clothed under the musty quilt, my back turned to him as he went on talking and stroking.

'This is nice,' I said.

We lay and told each other stories until I fell asleep. He told the story of a film he'd seen, about a young man and woman running away, he didn't say from what, and the man getting excited imagining them living in exotic locations, finally settling on a shack in China. The woman took on this stony look and described them hating each other in a horrible tenement, which must have been what really happened, because her look was like seeing the future and it's what you saw in the film, not them in his Chinese shack. I only wondered if he was describing Susan or some other woman. I fell asleep smiling.

He woke me up flustered, saying: 'We can't sleep here.' I didn't see why not. On the way back I was so sleepy I fell off my bike. We heard the phone ringing from outside the house. It was Susan, ringing to say goodnight, he said. 'She could have rung your mobile. I see. Checking up on us.' Though why it was worse for us to spend the night together in one place than in another I couldn't work out. But Susan had worked it out. Alistair said goodnight to me and closed the door of his room.

Most of all, she likes dressing me up. Half of what she

brought was clothes. If I see her in something I like, I just have to say, and she takes it off immediately. That's how I ended up in her roses dress in front of the dressing table mirror, blowing kisses to an imaginary Alistair. But because her feet are so big, I either have to wear her shoes like a girl dressing up or clump around in my boots. Dresses with boots might be all right in a squat, but not these dresses. I've wondered if she has money other than Alistair's – if she's rich. She doesn't do anything that I can see.

She does have taste though. She's not toying with me like I toyed with a school friend once, when I'd put make-up on her and do her hair. The weird thing is that it seems to be only for inside. She's happy for the world to go on seeing me in my blue parka and boots. No, not quite. She dressed me for a party. The people weren't exactly her friends – I can imagine what *they'd* be like – and at least didn't have to speak English with me. Though, of course, mostly they did. They love to.

I am careful with what I say about clothes, her appearance, careful generally. But I don't have to lie, except about the most important thing, and *he* is almost never around. His job is taking off. I think in fact he finds it hard being around us both. I milk Susan for stories about him, then get angry when they're about *them*. I know how hard his sister Catherine's death hit him, and what his mother was like (mad), and how he sharp-tongued his father into an early grave. I'm exaggerating. I find it all out while saying her hair looks better half-down, that her knees are wonderful and she suits red. She sees through me and I see her seeing through me. We are almost best friends.

I could laugh. Every night I've thought of taking the bread knife from the cutlery drawer and slashing her throat. I can't think beyond this point. I couldn't slip in beside Alistair over her bloody corpse. Anyway, I don't want to think. The moment of killing her is enough.

6

At the party she took me to, you could see everything through the top I wore. I enjoyed watching the men try not to look. Susan seemed just as much at ease with the women, whereas I find men nicer. She didn't mess up once. She introduced me as her husband's keeper, not caring how anyone took that.

I couldn't take my eyes off her. Her main technique is arching her back. She has to be in position first. That means on all fours on the floor or half-spread across a sofa or just kneeling, turning her head to speak to someone behind her. Her arms are important in all this, like the legs of a tripod or an easel, spreading her out till she's balanced perfectly, ending at the starfish of one hand flat on a surface. I'm not making a cartoon out of her – this is what she does.

I was able to follow her from where I stood in a doorway. This allowed a view of both main rooms and an adjoining kitchen. One of the rooms seemed to be for working in, maybe an architect's room – I didn't find out, though it would fit the bill. There was going to be a slideshow at some point. I spoke to one person who lived there. She kept me posted on her seduction of a boy fresh out of school. I liked her.

All the others I spoke to were men. The oldest, a well-scrubbed monster, ran a software company and had a 'teacher' who, he said, laid hands on him. 'Touch is so important. *Disinterested* touch is very healing.' I watched Susan watch me while she ate an open sandwich. Clever Susan. My monster drifted abstractly to the next body.

'You are that woman's husband's keeper,' said an oily voice in my ear.

It had oozed from another business type, more distinguished-looking, despite the corduroys in place of the full suit. I warmed to him and even pressed my side into him. He told me about his daughter and about his mistress, actually using that word, before asking about 'that woman' and her husband. I said lamely that my lips were sealed.

'I'm glad to report that you are in no respect her inferior,' he said.

'I'll say,' I said.

I wondered why Susan would want to be there, but I suppose she was comfortable in those surroundings. The places I'd been since moving back to the city, even though they were filled with the liberated, were a bit sexless I admit. If a man made a wrong move, you'd say something so caustic it could ruin him. I specialised in this.

The small red kitchen was the centre of things, with the two women hosts fussing over food and an Englishman making punch. 'No show without Punch,' he said to each guest who arrived. This made me smile, every time.

'Here we call Punch Jan Klassen,' I told him, loudly over the music.

'And Judy?'

'Katrijn. But I had an English puppet theatre as a girl.'

'Try some of this,' he said, and ladle-fed me some of the drink. 'Too much cough medicine?'

I ended up lying in the space on the bed for coats, where I could rest – I'd been sleeping even worse than usual lately – and pretend to eye up the men for Susan's sake. I knew I was being watched. Maybe they thought I would rifle through the pockets.

After a while I let my eyelids close and just listened. One voice, an American woman's, droned on about the poor quality TV and the lack of good classifieds. I looked to see if she was how I imagined her. She was blonde and glamorous, ageing visibly, the kind of woman you can't imagine sober. The man she was with was drunk too. At one point he caught me looking. I smiled over in sympathy.

'Missy, don't be sick on my coat,' the blonde called out. She moved like lightning to the bed. 'You look different from everybody else. Why don't we get you a real drink?'

She careered off. I only saw her once more – sitting on the toilet when I walked in on her. Her man, meanwhile, was fondling any woman in range.

'Let's go home, Susan,' I said. She was outside on the stairs with someone, smoking.

'But Alistair will be here any minute. He rang.'

'Oh, OK, I'll wait.'

I felt ugly. Not just me. Everyone made me think of woodlice. I so wanted Alistair to arrive.

He arrived with the smell of woodsmoke on him – in his clothes and his hair. I smelled it when he put his head to mine and asked how I was. I didn't look well. In all innocence he asked if Susan was neglecting me.

'*You're* neglecting me,' I said – and wanted to stop him unfastening that big coat of his and sob into it. He seemed a bit stunned.

'Let's go out into the garden,' he said. 'I've something to tell you.'

In the garden he gave me a hug – odd for him – and said he had gone to my old place today.

'I wanted to photograph it in daylight. There was someone there.'

'The owner.'

'Yes. He was putting your things into a skip. I've rescued everything – got a van from college to take it to our flat. It's all there.'

'He went through everything?'

'He said the builders would be starting work on it now. Don't be bitter. Everything's fine and back at our place. It was lucky I was there.'

I hadn't known how to end the part of my life before I had

met Alistair. Now it had been ended for me, I was too numb to feel anything.

'How will there be room for everything in the flat?'

'Susan and I will be moving out in a week's time. Don't worry. We can afford to keep both apartments going.'

It was too much. I said so and he said, 'Not at all.' Right now it was all too much.

'Can you take me back? Cycle with me. Leave Susan.'

'Let me just show my face at this party.'

I saw an opening in the trees, but he wouldn't be led. He called me a forest animal then contradicted himself, saying I couldn't escape being human so easily. He hugged me again as a parting gesture but I held onto him. Susan was looking down from the tall kitchen window. Her hand was like a lid flapping slowly over her glass, as she waved her fingers up and down – a slow, anxious wave.

7

Now they are on Prince's Canal where poor Anne Frank lived. I sleepwalked through the day they moved. I don't remember offering help, but I was soon carrying as much as Alistair while Susan instructed us. The van driver looked strangely at me, smilingly. I can't stand to be sneered at and I gave him the iciest stare you could imagine.

They are on three levels now. An old scrambled woman on the floor below kept popping out like a cuckoo from a clock. Susan will find some way of moving her on. Some nicest of ways. We hoisted everything up to what will be their living room and then I left.

I was back in the flat two hours when the phone rang. He said to meet him – I made him say why. Susan had insisted on taking the junk left by the owner and storing it in what was my place now. I felt the room spin. But he spoke so seductively that I said all right. 'Meet me at the 12 tram stop,' he said, 'and we'll take a bus out to a van hire place. It's not far. We let the other guy go before we thought of it.'

'Good,' I said, and meant 'good'. I don't think I'd have survived that night alone.

We had a long wait at the stop, too long. He didn't say much. I used the excuse of the night air to pant and lessen the silence, telling myself he had been quiet like this in the beginning too. It was good to stand next to him and watch the side of his face. He was if anything more beautiful in profile, imperious I suppose, like Caesar on a coin.

'This place is a bit of an oddity,' he said. 'I thought it could feature in our story of you. See what you think. It doubles as a barber's shop.'

It seemed an age since he'd spoken about the film.

The only odd thing from the outside was the red swirl of the writing. The left-hand side was a hairdresser's, the right a barber's, complete with miniature barber's pole. The door set a bell jangling.

A smell of smoke greeted us, followed by a tall German-looking blond man who moved to a desk. The girl sitting on the desk – not beautiful, but she clearly thought she was – ignored us.

The German lit a cigarette. 'I have bad news for you,' he said. 'The guy who has the van just phoned to say he'll be late back with it. It's a pisser for me too. I want to be lying on my sofa drinking my cocoa. What a day. You smoke?'

Alistair smiled his way through the banal small-talk that quickly dried up. The girl started haranguing the German on some point. It was good-natured, I suppose, if sex is good-natured. I saw the strategy in her approach. He was either indifferent or he was trying to look indifferent to hide some turmoil brought on by her. I know about this stuff.

The German photocopied Alistair's passport (its photo is of him in a black turtle-neck with face set grimly like a terrorist's) while we joked about taking the toy zebra on wheels instead. That wasn't even the most comical thing there. Oddly, the most comical belonged in a barber's: a child-sized cut-out of a barber with scissors poised and moustache almost bristling. I thought of those funfair rides where you measure yourself against a cartoon figure to be let on. This midget barber was a Casanova, clearly: you could see it in his eyes. When Alistair leaned on him like a small friend, I laughed. The girl scowled. I wanted to remove her cigarette and slap her.

'Do you have a toilet I could use?' Alistair asked. He had a polite voice for all the wrong occasions. If the German and his girl hadn't turned my stomach already, they did now, launching jointly on a description of why the toilet was out of use.

A big old-fashioned cash register was propped on a stand with a doily underneath it. Those two morons were still talking. I fingered the doily's brown waves of dirt and opened the money drawer. I hadn't expected there to be money inside, but there was – a lot of it. This was some place.

I've had to scavenge in my time but I never actually stole money. Now I wanted to take this and walk out the door, away from Alistair and everything. He'd see that he'd picked up a street whore who just couldn't help herself. How Susan would comfort him too. 'There, there. Leopards don't change their spots. I knew from the first.'

Alistair came back and I joined him at the window. The rain was bringing umbrellas out onto the street. Bad weather for moving. I tugged on his sleeve, made him look at an old reel-to-reel and projector high up on a shelf. 'A sign,' I said, thinking of our film, but he only smiled. Near the beaded curtain at the back, a long paddle like a propeller was secured to the wall. Above it, a sign saying *Saltash*.

For Alistair, this dead place with its dead things signified me. Worse, he was here, inside his idea of me, and not even looking around.

Eventually the van trundled into view. The German inspected it with a thin metallic torch. I was glad to be in the raised seat beside Alistair – I like the smell of vans somehow, especially on a rainy night when a blast of warm air hits the seats.

'They're obviously lovers,' I said of the odd couple we'd just left, 'but he's losing interest in her. Or maybe he never was interested in her.'

'You think so?'

I had to goad him into speaking his mind.

'She's the friend of his younger sister,' he said, 'and likes to hang out with him, wants him to make a move on her, but he's not sure. He's weighing it up, but he can't think straight. Is she too young? What would his friends say? Is lying on his sofa drinking cocoa enough for a young girl?'

'I still say they're lovers.'

'But what did you think of the place?' he asked after a silence.

'A pile of crap.'

I'd had to look at Bohemian junk in the past till it was coming out my ears. That was squat territory all right. I never knew what I was supposed to say. They'd hand you a colourful kaleidoscope or a small stringed instrument and expect your world to be instantly changed. I'd nod and pass it along like a joint. So Alistair had me pegged as that type.

'If I put a camera in your place, do you promise to record yourself?' he asked.

'Record myself doing what?'

'We don't have to go into the details. Tell me about your life, make up another life, as long as you stay in front of the camera. I'll set the camera up on a tripod for you. *You* gave me the idea, you know, with that roll of film of yourself just walking along. You seemed very animated.' He had asked me to take photographs of the city and I had.

'I didn't develop that film,' I said.

'No, but I did.'

'And it inspired you?'

'You don't know how much. I'd wanted you to capture the city for me, then I understood – you *are* this city.'

'I am?'

'Will you do it?'

I said yes, a little sullenly, confused that he seemed one

minute not to care and the next to have all these designs on me. Maybe he'd even worked this out at the barber's while I was thinking I only disappointed him.

I explained to him how I felt about that place, speaking of the kaleidoscopes and stringed instruments, which amused him.

'You don't know that crowd,' I said, trying hard to drive the point home. 'You never had to live constantly watching what you said. They wanted you to fuck up exactly like they'd fucked up. They were so proud of their abortions.'

8

Susan came round. I was busy picking scabs off Bibi – he's caught something, I don't know what. I wish I'd been painting my toenails instead. All the while we talked, the little saucer with the scabs lay at her feet. I tried not to look at it.

'Are you hungry?' I asked. 'I could cook you something.'

'You're too sweet. Actually I am hungry.'

I made her a perfect omelette the way Alistair showed me.

'Femke,' she said, finally, 'I'm here on an errand. Of Alistair's.'

'Oh yeah?'

'I have some equipment of his for filming you. I'm so happy you agreed to do it. It was my idea, you know. Did he tell you?'

'Of course.'

'Yes, he would tell you. He holds you in very high esteem.'

I knew she was buttering me up, but I couldn't conceal my joy.

'As do I,' she smiled.

I mumbled something ungrammatical in praise of them both, which only broadened her smile.

'Now, where shall we set things up? Alistair suggested the sideboard.'

I would empty the day's rubbish from my jeans on top of this sideboard. I saw her inspecting it all as she helped clear it away. What would she discover? From the fast-food receipts that I hate cooking for just myself. That I've taken to crossing the city by tram not foot.

She made me sit in the big old-lady armchair, facing the sideboard. She focused the camera then repositioned me, picking stray hairs off the antimacassar. I did a sound test by humming Norwegian Wood. What a tune! I would gladly be turned to ashes with that tune playing.

'You can whisper if you like, it'll still pick you up.'

'I can't see me sitting here whispering, can you?'

'No, Femke,' she laughed. 'I can't.'

And that was it. She left me an instruction manual in English 'just in case'. But I know how to press a few buttons. How to press hers.

The next time we met was when she came for the tape and inserted a new one. That would have been the Monday morning. Start of the week. She was working now, in television, scheduling programmes. I didn't ask which channel. I've enough entertainment in my life without TV.

'How did the two of you meet?' The words spilled out like spaghetti from a toddler's mouth. From my mouth. I had never even asked Alistair. He wouldn't have answered anyway, except with a lie and a sideways smile.

'That's a very good question,' she said.

'Is it?'

She gave me a sharp look and I thought, *Steady, steady*.

'I used to be a barmaid…' she began.

'*You* were a barmaid?'

'Is that so surprising?'

I could have kicked myself.

'Not really,' I said. 'Just that you're so… glamorous now.'

'But barmaids *are* glamorous, by and large.'

'Not here they're not,' I said, still not shutting up.

'This was in London town.' (She said *town* oddly, more like *tan*.) 'A pub in the East End, if that means anything to you. A funny name – The Barrister's Wig. Must have been in honour of all the lawyers who got rich on its customers' lifestyles. Oh dear, you do look puzzled.'

'Not puzzled, listening.'

'Right. The landlord had a certain fondness for the upper halves of his female staff. You get me? He was a very persuasive man, and the girls would let themselves be photographed topless for him. For him and his wife, actually – they had a sort of photo-montage on their bedroom wall.'

'That's disgusting,' I said. 'Where does Alistair come in?'

'Oh he came in a while back. He was the photographer.'

'No.'

'I kid you not.'

'And you? Did you?'

'I did,' she said, laughing and leaning in to me. 'I can't say I'm proud of it now. But everything seems harmless at that age. It's funny to see you so shocked. Alistair needed the cash, I needed the job, and, Alistair being Alistair, the photos were actually very good. It was almost like being a model. You think he's charming now – you should have heard him back then. He could charm the birds out of the trees.'

So I was just another bird, charmed out of the trees, by a charmer who was losing it.

'And you've been together ever since?'

'After a bit, yes. The first thing I made him do was stop taking those bloody photos.'

'Was yours pinned up too?'

'I never found out. I'm sure it was. I was only in the bedroom once, by mistake. Oh Femke, that's a thought! I might still be there.'

I had to give her a hand getting the tape into the machine. Clearly she was no help to Alistair in his work, so why this pretence?

'Was Alistair pleased with my tape?'

'Yes, he was. He seemed very pleased.'

'Did he say so?'

'You know Alistair. You have to… *interpret* happiness in him.'

Well, I knew exactly what she meant, but I wasn't going to give her the pleasure of hearing me admit that I, too, couldn't make him happy in a straightforward way. I think she understood this. I think the look she gave me then was a pitying one.

'Were *you* pleased with my tape?'

'Now, now, that's naughty of you. You're only fishing to see if I watched it. I did, as a matter of fact. I think it's simply brilliant. Perhaps in the next tape – this is only *my* suggestion – perhaps you could give a bit more of yourself. Less description of Bibi and her day and more about you, your day, all your days – from way back. I'm sure there's an interesting story to tell. I might be saying the wrong thing here. Alistair might want more of a diary type thing after all. No, just ignore me, and do what feels right. You'll know yourself when you're on the right track.'

She pressed some money – a hundred-guilder note – into my hand as she left. I was too stunned to give it back. What was this? What was happening now?

I put the money on the sideboard, tucked just under the video camera. Why not? If this was her payment – or his – for the tape I'd made, that's where it belonged. If I made enough tapes then the piles of cash would push the camera higher and higher. Eventually they'd see only my head, then nothing at all. The wall opposite. What was on it? Alistair's sister, Catherine. The dead one.

Ever since she left I've been unable to settle to anything. Bibi looks at me with the same pitying look I saw *her* give. All right, that's an exaggeration. But he's lost some life from his eyes. Maybe it's time to resume our walks. I don't know. Could he be missing Alistair? But Alistair was only ever attentive in fits and starts. Ain't that the truth.

I've turned to the junk rescued from the skip. Most of it is kept in shoeboxes, surprisingly, as I've never been one for hoarding shoes. Or is that it: I threw out the shoes but kept the boxes? It doesn't matter. Except that it throws me how little attention I've paid to these things. To what it is I've been doing all these years.

There isn't any chronology involved, so it's as well to pick a box at random. This one dates back to 92. I know because of the train ticket – not from the date, as it's illegible now, so much so I think the ticket must have been through a wash. No, I know because that was the year I arrived here, the only one in which I still travelled home. That much is legible. I say 'home'.

I'm no thief, but there are times when I am unable to return things. Like this friendship bracelet. An English girl called Emily owned it. She gave me the bracelet, not to keep, but as a charm to ward off the panic I felt when I left the squat. It was only ever fleeting – once I realised the streets were a friendlier place than the squat, I got over it. Emily disappeared or else caught the panic herself: once I'd moved out, I never saw her again. So that's not theft. How thin she must have been to wear this. How thin I was, in 92.

Nothing else means much to me now. I can't even think why

I kept a commemorative coin of Beatrix and Claus's 25th. And I don't know whose phone number is scrawled on this Rizla packet – it might be fun to call it some time. I do remember collecting numbers at parties and binning them afterwards. Nice to get a reputation for being a slut without actually having to be one.

The tape she came for today will likely be my last. I've said all there is to say already, feel like I'm at a cliff edge almost. It's terrifying to come to the end of yourself.

9

How do I start this?

How end it?

Well, it's over, that's clear. That's crystal clear. Ah, he got me, he really did. He must be very proud of himself to have got me so bloody whole and exact. It was a clever plan, cleverly executed.

The director's cut.

To think I thought I had talked myself out. The talk is only starting.

One more tape. I'll get it ready in a bit.

But I must stop my hands from trembling. I must find a dead calm inside.

Father.

So it was like this. I started again on my rounds, taking Bibi to see the burnt-church offices and the boys, ordering an Americano from the coffee cart. Everything was exactly as it was yet nothing seemed the same. I am no detective, but I knew what this meant: I had changed.

Bibi perked up, though, and I found myself saying 'Good boy' and realising I hadn't told him this in a while. You can imagine my guilt. I loosened my grip and let him lead the way. We went round in circles like that till I thought of our old place. I had an urge to go there, to see it obliterated and know my past was at an end.

When I saw that it hadn't changed, I still didn't suspect. *That lazy landlord,* I thought. I would have turned on my heel but Bibi strained to go closer. Then I saw a figure flit across the glass.

The figure of a woman or a girl. I was curious now – maybe there is a bit of the detective in me after all. But what could I do? I could hardly knock. Nobody had ever knocked on that rusty old door all the while I was there. Even Alistair had only fallen against it.

If you hesitate for long enough, someone will always decide for you. And so the door opened and a girl-like woman came out with a saucepan in her hand, tipped the contents into the water, and looked at me oddly, like someone trying to read without their reading glasses.

'Are you visiting me?' she asked.

'I used to live here,' I said. 'With my dog.'

'Oh, so you're feeling nostalgic. Come in and have a look.'

Her hair was long and black, like mine, only less tangled. I resisted an impulse to touch it.

Inside was different all right. Only now could I see how spartanly I'd furnished the place. Here was the sort of dross I'd told Alistair about, the paraphernalia of every hippie chick. I sat in a hanging chair that didn't hang but lay propped in the corner.

'Chamomile or rooibus?' she asked.

'Rooibus.'

She heated the water on the two-ring gas hob I knew so well, using the saucepan she'd just emptied.

'How long ago were you here?'

'A few months.'

'So recently? You must have been the last one here then. Before me, I mean.'

'I was told it was being demolished.'

'Really? Who told you that?'

'The landlord. Not directly.'

'I never met him.'

Bibi disappeared into the alcove. I looked around, not taking anything in. I was thinking about something without knowing what.

'I must say, I love it. The sound of the water at night is so lulling. Didn't you find that?'

'Bibi didn't.'

'Bibi? Oh, your dog. She's lovely?'

'She's a he.'

'I have a friend called Bibi, isn't that funny? But she's most definitely a she.'

'My mother gave him that name. I like it now.'

'Look at him nosing around. He seems happy to be here…
Here you go.'

'Thanks.'

We drank our tea in silence for a bit.

'That was nice, thanks.' I really didn't know what to say to
her.

'What's your name?' she asked, finally.

'Femke.'

'No! What a coincidence!'

'You're Femke too?'

'No,' she said, a look of puzzlement intensifying on her face.
I was so puzzled myself it was like looking in a mirror.

'Do you know a man called Alistair, by any chance?'

My skin caught fire. Now my eyes focused on what they
had been looking at: one of Alistair's video lights I'd unpacked
from a crate that time.

'I know Alistair,' I said.

'You should have said before. Did he tell you to come here?'

'I haven't spoken to him for weeks. I don't know anything
about you. I only came to look at my old place.'

'All right, it's all right. I believe you.' (Did she think I was
about to burst into tears? Maybe I was.) 'It's me who should
explain, then. I'm taking Alistair's film course. He set me up
here – he's old-fashioned like that. I like old-fashioned men.
He's making a short called *Femke* and I'm playing the lead part.
I say that, but it's the only part. We're filming it in stages. Each

week he brings me a new piece of the script. He doesn't like me to know too much in advance. Some directors work that way, you know.'

'Can I see the script?'

'Sure. He lets me keep the instalments. I'm supposed to read them before he gives me the next one, but I never do. Don't tell him that. Am I playing you? Is that what this is about?'

'Didn't he say?'

'I never asked. I thought it was just a part he made up. He said I was perfect for it.'

She handed me the last 'instalment' and, as I knew I would, I read my own words there, from my own last instalment.

'Is it your story?' she asked.

'No,' I said, handing back the loose sheets.

I took hold of Bibi and let myself out. She came to the door anyway, calling out after me: 'Don't be a stranger.'

I left in a kind of panic, like in the old days, when I'd be holed up in the squat for weeks. Only I was outside, chugging breath out of my lungs and moving fast. So fast, Bibi was pulling me back. I walked all the way out west, till the monotony of Admiral de Ruyter Road started to placate me. I still couldn't think what any of it meant. All I could do was relive the meeting, see and hear all again, from the quizzical look she gave as she tipped out the contents of the pan (what was in it? water from the alcove?) to the blurted words at my back. Was I anything but a stranger? Would I ever be anything but a stranger, to anyone?

And it all fell into place, the detail I missed without, in fact, missing any of it. Such as my hearing 'rooibus' when what she said was 'red bush', just as Alistair called it. I could see the features of her face and understand why these spelled Femke to him, the Femke he had wanted me to be. That thin scar above her left eye. I've no blemish on my skin, despite all my rough living: this puzzled him. And her girlish appearance. He liked the appearance of rough living but not the extra years it etches on your face. Even Susan, come to think of it, dressed girlishly. Those short floral dresses. The pink make-up.

I'd recovered my breath and was walking more surely, stopping at the tram stop and knowing where I was headed. When the tram came I got on at the front and looked straight at the driver. I think I will see his face when I'm on my deathbed – some moods fix things like that. The tourists who got off at the same stop parted to let me past.

It was the middle of the day, so probably only Susan would be home – I didn't believe a word about her job in television. I had nothing to say to her. I had nothing to say to him. Yet my legs strode on as if a magnet pulled them. I stopped at the curiosity shop and looked up: no figure moved across the glass.

I rang the doorbell with my heart in my mouth. No answer. Susan was lazy, though, and might be inside, waiting for me to go. I rang again, and waited again. Then I turned the handle of the door, but they weren't so careless as to leave it unlocked.

So I did what they do in the movies, and barged the door with my shoulder.

No joy.

This was ridiculous, but so what? There was no one there to ridicule me.

They were careless after all, and very English: the key was under the mat.

I hadn't been here since the day of the move. Now I thought of that poor girl's verdict of Alistair, which I'd dismissed at the time. Old-fashioned. How had I managed not to notice before? There was the hat stand, and the hall mirror, and the shoe rack, all in matching mahogany.

I didn't come to hesitate in the hall.

I looked in the living room and in the kitchen, but there was no sign of anything. Then I followed a kind of coconut-oil smell that took me to their bedroom. With its king-size bed. The bed faced a TV with a video-recorder propped on top, and a stack of videos on the left-hand side. Hitchcocks and Antonionis and Bergmans: Alistair's usual fare. They were all shop-bought. Then I looked under the bed.

Alongside the dirty socks – hers and his – was a stash of video porn. (Oh Alistair, this wasn't what *we* got up to at night, remember?) In amongst it, a video marked 'F'.

I switched on the TV and slotted the video into the machine. After a few seconds my face appeared – pieces of my face, coming together finally. I turned up the volume but there was no sound. What day was this? Which instalment? I saw from my top that it was the first day. It wasn't right, though – too choppy. Stop-start.

Then I got it. Everything had been cut, apart from my trances. I had never seen one before, it was quite something. So that was what all the tests and the hospital spider plants had been about. My head drooping slightly, like I was nodding off, but my eyes still open. Sometimes my mouth moved like I was speaking – I tried the volume again, it was cranked right up. Nothing. Then my clothes changed, meaning it was into another day, and more trances. The whole tape like that. Lasting what – three minutes, four? It felt like a lifetime.

I left the tape in the machine. Let them find out. Let them come home and find the door lying open and fear the worst and check their valuables and breathe easy again, and then, last thing, let them find the tape in the machine and let it dawn on them. Let it dawn on them like it dawned on me, so they know I know. Let them know I know they know I know.

10

Forget all I said. I am a liar, born to it. You want to hear the truth? You want to hear it?

All right, twelve is good. You would have liked me at twelve. You would have stayed with me.

My daddy didn't. He left for America on my twelfth birthday. How's that for a slap across the jaw? No, no lies here, it was the night before my birthday, I was asleep at the time. I could sleep then.

I know he went to America because I found a letter from there, from him, in Mother's dressing table. Inside the velvet lining of her jewellery box. He had written about always taking care of me and winding up the business. I can believe he wound up the business.

But you don't want to hear about that. You want to hear about the other thing. Well, you're just going to have to wait.

It was a school day, I remember that too. And she made me go, even as she cried for him, bent double on the orange sofa. 'He's gone! He's gone!' one minute, and 'Go! Go!' the next. So I went. I was shaking all day. I sat in the toilet cubicle looking at my trembling hands. Imagine that. Imagine it.

He had left for America. A plane had taken him there, and a plane could bring him back. When I learnt from Mother's phone calls that he'd left with his white-gloved secretary, I thought: *He'll soon get tired of her.*

After that, it became a waiting game. I am good at games. I play to win.

Not so fast. There's the small business of my birthday cake. Mother lit the twelve candles with her cigarette lighter. Her hands trembled as much as mine did, more so. I could have told her to stop but I wanted the candles lit. (Had she been practising? The wicks were already black.)

Mother cancelled the party-tea invitations to my handful of friends – the ones she thought were my friends – and we ate the cake alone, in silence. Come to think of it, I was the only one eating.

I started fitting after that. Full-blown seizures. Grand mal – there's a dignity to the French. Then the fits changed, got less bad but more frequent. Partial, they called them. No dignity in that.

If only he could have seen me like that he would have come back surely. I'd upped the stakes in the game. But how to get a message through to him? Write to America! Yes, I could see him in his white wooden house, big hands calmly opening the airmail envelope. 'What is it, darling?' 'Oh nothing,' he says, folding it away in an inside pocket of his suit before heading straight to the airport.

Then I had a brainwave. I wrote my own letter – more of a note, really, saying 'Come back' – and put it in with his, taped the letter closed, wrote 'Return to Sender' on it, like in the song, and posted it. Now I didn't even have his letter to look at.

My fits made me a star at school. I could tell that the people who shunned me were in awe of me. The person who shunned me least was Suzan Swart. Nothing could take her from my side.

I liked dressing her up. This was after school, in her bedroom. I did her hair and make-up too, till she looked really crazed. All that blue and yellow above the eyes, and black below. Hair like a distressed poodle.

I couldn't get her to leave the room, though. She would do anything for me except leave that room. Her mum was forever bringing beakers of lemonade and slices of butter cake, and frowning at Suzan's look. Still, we were in the house, I suppose. That's what mothers like.

In school she was my shadow. Yes, exactly like my shadow – taller in the morning than in the afternoon, after I'd cut her down to size. How did I do it? By every means possible. As well as fitting, I'd started smoking. And being tall I could stand with the smokers at the gate. I even exchanged smoke with the boys there. First kisses. All of this mortified Suzan. I kept my eyes open while I kissed, watching her watch me. Poor Suzan.

I knew from Mother what to look for. The sunken eyes, the torpor. That dead slowness performing the simplest task.

I stopped the torment at this point: her descent had its own momentum now. In less than a month she was out of the school, and my life, for good.

The surprise was that I missed her company, especially in the breaks. I had to conspire all the time to look busy, on my way somewhere. Only if I dawdled would it look like loneliness.

At thirteen there wasn't a birthday cake. There never would be one again. I wasn't any more the girl who curled up with Mother at matinee movie time.

Things only got worse at school. This time I reserved the torment for the teachers, which won me admirers if not friends. Eventually I decided to introduce an element of real danger, and switched on a gas tap as I left the science class. No explosion, just an evacuation. They couldn't pin it on me, but they had no doubt. I was never allowed to be last to leave again.

It might have gone on like this forever if a boy hadn't blown sweet-tasting smoke into my mouth. I tried a few joints after that, but they didn't have the desired effect, which was to make me not be me. Still, they were currency. The trouble was, I was so out of the loop with other people that I couldn't source a good supply. So I bought what I could from that goofy boy and sold it on, at a small loss. I didn't care. I just wanted to be the one to come to.

Word soon got out, as I knew it would.

So began the worst phase of my life, when Mother escaped the shame by dragging me to the suburbs. 'An oasis of tranquillity,'

I expect the estate agent said. It was dead all right.

The world is run by the dead. A wise man taught me that. But it's too soon to bring *you* into the story.

I suppose these *were* the men who ran the world – in their own eyes, at least. They went into the city and left their wives behind. Not that their wives stayed behind for long. After a year or two of crushing boredom, they (crushed) resumed their careers, or found new ones. A tidy little supplementary income.

Does this sound overly bitter? Does it?

You see, I grew up quick after Father's abandonment. A beautiful widow and her pubescent daughter are not nothing. The men didn't tempt me, but then, they didn't have to. I had a cure for the softness of their home lives.

Mother, meanwhile, had taken up her old job of hairdressing at home. One or two made the trip from the city, but most of the customers were new. I opened the door to them. The ones who knew me said how unrecognisable I was, and then in the next breath that I'd been a lovely child.

Whatever living she made from this was small change next to the outgoings we had. Clearly, our suburban idyll was being subsidised by Father, yet his name never passed our lips.

I was desperate to get back to the city.

How did I meet him – the man who took away my innocence? (Don't laugh.) He was sitting on a park bench. That's where the devil always sits.

There must have been some opening gambit, but it escapes me. I let it escape me.

Whatever was said, I was soon sitting alongside him. This wasn't so unusual. I passed the time of day with all sorts. He had a worldly air I found appealing. (You have it too.) It was just a conversation, and at the end of it he got up and walked away. But he looked back, and saw that I was still looking at him. Which made him smile. Have you seen the devil smile? The first time you see it you know you've seen it before, but where?

I suppose I could have moved, found another park, maybe even another squat far enough away. But every day he was there I was there too. I felt drawn to him. Like when a bluebottle beats itself against a window-pane in your room and you know you should let it out and you don't move because you're hypnotised by the buzzing, by being in the company of something so ugly.

Once or twice he laid his hand on my hand on the park bench, but I moved mine away, saying, 'I think not.' So he knew he couldn't go down that route with me. I did, though, accept the occasional meal. Nothing fancy, just some hot snacks out of Febo's, meaning his largesse consisted of putting coins into the slots of little food windows. And since the food in them is suitable for dogs too, Bibi also got fed. I had taken Bibi with me to the city.

I never once asked what he was after. Some part of me knew already, but it still came as a shock when he put it to me plainly, saying: 'There are men who would pay good money to be with you.' I had just bitten down on a chicken wing and couldn't chew. Sat there with my mouth full of teeth.

'What you did in the suburbs was nothing. Nothing,' he said, with a wave of his hand. I suppose he was absolving me so that I could do worse with a clean slate. 'This would be real money. You could do it for six months and not have to work again for three years. I know a very clean place, very discreet. A private house, where even the clients never get to see one another.'

I thought suddenly of Father, pictured him climbing a secret wooden staircase to his white-gloved whore. I hadn't noticed how sick my head had become.

'I don't feel well,' I said, sinking into his chest.

'You're all right,' he said, stroking my hair, his fingers digging into my scalp. 'You're all right.'

I started work on the Monday, just as if it was a regular job. The madam was a small Chinese man who never smiled. He showed me my room, and where the towels and sheets were kept, and how to load the washing machines. It was like starting work in a laundry. But then he took me back to my room and went over the menu and the prices. He asked if I was comfortable with everything on the menu and I said yes. I said yes to get him out of the room. He opened a drawer full of condoms and then left for a while. I sat down on the bed.

It was all only a dream, so where was the harm? And I could

walk away at any point. Vincent – that was the devil's name – had told me this as he left me at the door. Though I had a suspicion that if I did walk he would find me. And he had Bibi, for today at least. I decided I would work for a week and then find a place for Bibi and me, not the room Vincent put me in, above the tobacconist. The lower you descend, the smaller the space you are given. So it goes.

My first client was a boy in his 20s, very sullen. He grunted when I asked him to wash beforehand. I hadn't spoken to the other girls yet, and didn't know they wouldn't always insist on this. I tried to make him come quickly, which only annoyed him more. He was going to get value for money, in time if not pleasure. When he came he withdrew immediately, so I didn't have a hold of the base of the condom like I'd been told. There was spillage on my leg and the sheet. This excited him, but his half-hour was up. He would have paid for another go, I'm sure.

I put my head out of the window and smoked a cigarette. Before I could finish it, I had to pull my head in and join the walk-by parade in the lobby. Luckily the guy didn't choose me. I must have had a frown on my face.

This time I went back to my room and lit up again, but soon I was flitting in and out of the rooms of the other girls who'd just been rejected, talking like I'd never talked before. Not being chosen was a drag for some of the girls – two of them had young kids, and needed to make the time count – but I welcomed it. I got to know everybody's life story, each a million times more colourful than mine, so of course I had to invent a little. They were wise to me, laughing at my ignorance of the world. (Like you laughed, though I knew a lot more by then.)

I got to the end of the week and I got my place but I didn't stop working. It was old Mrs Bijl – you remember her – who sorted me out. She looked me over like she smelled my work on me, but softened at the sight of Bibi. It was a basement flat, even smaller than Vincent's offering, but I knew I had to cut my ties to him. First the flat, and then the job. Only, not yet.

I broke down just the once. Mr Zang gave me the week off to recover. They were sad sweet days, spent with Bibi, in a place where nobody in the world knew I was, except for a crazy woman who fed mouldy bread to birds. I had one book of old nursery rhymes – I'd found it wedged between the cutlery drawer and the stove. I read the rhymes to Bibi, then quietly to myself.

Sail your boat, drink your tea.
We're sailing to the Overtoom,
Drinking sweet, sweet milk with cream.

That one's my favourite.

Eventually I relaxed a little in my work. Some of the men would ask for me, and they became my regular punters. Not many, but enough. I didn't feel the need to numb myself with tranquillisers either, though I never said no when offered, and put them in the drawer with the condoms. I was learning the ropes and trying, above all, not to look out of place. It was only for a short while anyway.

Then Bibi got depressed, cooped up in the flat all day. He would tear at the two-seater sofa that was already torn, and urinate in corners. I scolded him at first, but it wasn't the answer: it never is. I had to find a place where he could roam free in the day without ending up in a shelter. But before I could move, Mrs Bijl came round and caught sight of the damage: I tried speaking to her through a crack, but her booted foot wedged the door open. There was no reason for her to call, which made me suspect that she knew already, that she'd let herself in when I was out.

This was when I got my place near the harbour. You know, the place you emptied and lied about and installed my successor in. Bibi could roam the dock, and I could walk him properly in the evenings. It was perfect. It really was perfect.

This is where you come in.

This is where you come in, with your good coat with the collar turned up and scarf tied as only classy men know how. You'd think by now I wouldn't notice, that the faces in the lobby would be a blur, a succession of hungry stares with no detail worth recalling. Maybe that's true most of the time, but not now. I give you my straight look, and it hits the rose: you.

So you follow me up the stairs, clasping the hand I offer you. That's a nice touch, isn't it? Hinting at intimacy but really only a safety precaution. Those stairs are narrow, right? You follow me, and I know you're breathing me in, my scent isn't cheap like the other girls'. You see, I've started to invest in myself. In the landing I let go of your hand in case you get the wrong idea – in case you start to get the right idea. Because I do feel something, though the whole world swears I don't.

In the room you close the door. It should be me, but I let it happen. This is where I ask, 'What will it be, sweetie?', but the words won't come. Instead we look at each other a moment too long. This can't be happening, right? I am imagining it. You can't be feeling what I feel because I have a heavy cold that makes my nose red and makes me cough up phlegm that I swallow again. And right on cue you break the spell, telling me what it will be. Oh right. Like I haven't heard that a thousand times before.

I want this look to stay with you forever. I want you to remember it when you are with whoever you are with.

So it ends as it always ends, with the awkward afters. Strange, because the awkwardness left me ages ago, but here it is back again. Crazy me to have expected anything other than the 'Bye, then' you leave me with. And I mean crazy. Because I don't go with you but lie back down again and shout 'Next!' as nobody does. Next! Next! And the next man does come, not from the lobby but the landing, and he's – you.

Well that's you all over: letting me down and lifting me up again in almost the same moment.

This time I close the door.

PART TWO

A Muse to God

'This is his *life* mask,' the man in the shop said.

I was handing over the plaster bust of Beethoven that I'd promised Bibi for so long.

'My mistake,' I said. 'I thought it was done after his death. I'm sure I heard that.'

'There *was* a death mask made, but it's very different from this. He was a long time sick before he died.'

My attempts at haggling came to nothing. Maybe I was losing my touch.

'It's just as well for you that it's pay-day, boy,' I said to Bibi.

'It's for your *dog*?'

I like idling like this before work, letting the butterflies go wild in my stomach. If I leave it late enough there is always the possibility that I won't go in and my life will start to unravel again. Walking away from a cleaning job isn't everyone's idea of suicide, I know. But this is my flirtation now. Better to flirt with death than be married to it.

From the shop I crossed the street and filed past the market stalls. The sellers all knew not to waste their time on me, and I liked their no-nonsense talk. *Shit or get off the pot*, I could expect to hear as I sized up a plum. I would laugh in their faces, in a more friendly way than they thought. Why grouch about them? They were out to make a living in the only way they knew. And, besides, they were tired. Tired and defeated, some of them. This was the end of their working day, and the start of mine.

Only, not yet.

Bibi wasn't quite tired out, and I had to make sure he could last the next three hours alone in my room. It was a big blue south-facing room, in a flat of smaller north-facing rooms. I had charmed the couple who rented it out. They were dog lovers, and though I am not, strictly speaking, one of those (I am faithful to Bibi), I know enough about the species to pass an hour or two respectably among its lovers. The trouble was that they had already promised the room to someone, so there was friction from the start. But he was a boy who played his guitar all day, and I was nice to him about his playing, which I did enjoy, and he came out of his sulk eventually, and even helped me paint the room. I was once told never to paint a bedroom blue. But I don't always do what I'm told.

So I walked Bibi around the outskirts of the park, past my old house, past the museum, close to the zoo, and then back to the flat, avoiding the market this time. In the room he lay his head flat on the rug and watched me gather my things. Leaving, I blew him a kiss, as always.

The job in the burnt-church offices only came up a month

ago. I like it – there's more to it than toilets. The squarish teaching rooms hum pleasantly from the air-conditioning. Not too many tables and chairs. Carpet-tiled. I go in as the last class goes out, run a damp cloth over the surfaces, empty the bins, that sort of thing. If I do see people, they're always polite, which I mind less now. This day I walked into a class that had overrun its time. My eyes had to adjust to the light – Charlie Chaplin was on TV, and the blinds were closed. A standing man in a three-piece suit smiled at me, saying 'Not at all.' *Odd*, I thought, as I closed the door. A silent movie in a language school.

In the basement I bumped into Mohammed, the cleaner-in-chief. He quizzed me about my progress before handing over my pay in a small square envelope marked 'F'. I counted the money in front of him.

And that was the end of my shift. Arduous but short, and enough for now. Enough to keep a roof over our heads, to keep my head from drifting off. Because it does drift off still.

It was my aunt who suggested cleaning. She keeps a clean house herself – always has, she says. She told me the secret is not to wish you were somewhere else. Just clean, and take an interest in cleaning. There are some things you hear and immediately dismiss and then they creep back into your head again, when your head's on the pillow unable to rest. Her words were like that. What I am is nothing to be ashamed of.

Or it must be, for me to be so adamant. There – I've said it. I'm ashamed of the person I am.

I quickly rescued Bibi from the room. Out in the street the light was getting dark. It was cold, and the seats outside the brown cafes were empty. I walked for a bit under the orange glow of the streetlamps, but I had a hankering for green and decided to cut through the park.

It was down to Bibi what happened next.

He stopped at the feet of a man sitting on a bench next to the great bed of hyacinths. Normally, the overhanging branches of elm made this spot dark even in daylight. Bibi's interest, awkwardly enough, was in the dog shit on one of the man's boots. I saw him from his boots up, with my lip curled in faint disgust. But I smiled when I saw his hat – large and black, a flamboyant Spaniard's hat – and the white hair sticking out from under it. Here, plainly, was a character, not the usual park character with some sexual malaise to explain him.

'Come away,' I said, but Bibi was oddly defiant. Then the man filled the silence.

'Is that Beethoven you have in your hand? I can't tell in this light.'

'Yes, it is,' I said. I hadn't noticed the brown wrapping-paper hanging loose.

'I have a bust like that, of the Englishman William Blake.'

'Really?'

'You haven't heard of William Blake?'

'No.'

The man started singing.

'He wrote those words. Marvellous words. And a marvellous tune. Have you any idea how rare a combination that is?'

'I never thought about it.'

'Well, now you have.'

'I might not have,' I said, oddly defiant myself. 'I might just be being polite.'

He laughed at that, said, 'Sit yourself down,' while gesturing towards the space beside him. Despite my smiling confidence, I had to quickly gauge the danger.

'There's no danger,' he said. 'I am old. And *you* have a dog.'

'You're not that old.'

Close up, the hair below the hat brim resembled strands of white wire, and there were strands of the same wire sprouting from his nostrils. A zigzag scar on his forehead was like the fold in a certain kind of bread loaf. His skin was exceptionally white except for the colour in his cheeks, which looked like bruising in the poor light. He hadn't shaved since yesterday at least. His jaws were large, his lips and nose large also.

'I take it it's a he.'

'Yes, called Bibi. Don't ask.'

'The first secret between us,' he said, with an even stronger laugh.

Bibi lay quietly at my feet – at the man's feet, truth be told – but I kept hold of the lead, with not too firm a grip.

'My mother called him Bibi. She wasn't good at paying attention.'

'So, no secrets. Very good. And what would *you* have called him.'

'I don't know. I liked the name Shalimar for a while, less so now.'

'Pale hands I loved, beside the Shalimar,' he said in English. 'A bit pretentious for a dog.'

'That's what I thought.'

There was silence then, for a while. A good silence.

'Do you live nearby? I live nearby,' I found myself saying.

'Nearby, yes. On Transvaal Street. Do you know it?'

'I know all the streets round here. I spent my childhood here.'

'So this is your playground. Very good.'

'And you've been here... how long?'

'My childhood playground was very large indeed. I am the son of a diplomat, you see. But that's not what you asked. Forgive me. I lived here long ago, and then again, for the past... *two* decades. I can't see you very well, but I imagine two decades would almost cover the span of your existence. I don't recall having seen you here.'

'I didn't always look like this,' I said.

'No, of course not. You look very well, by the way.'

'Thank you.'

'And I?'

'Well, you didn't frighten Bibi.'

He bent over then, laughing as if in pain. The laughter caused him to cough, which seemed to cause him to reach inside his coat, a black mackintosh. He was soon struggling to light a cigarette.

'A Marlboro man,' I said, holding the lighter steady.

'Just my small obeisance to the culture of America,' he said. 'I worked out long ago that whatever is going to happen, good or bad, is bound to happen there first. This commands a certain respect. If not love.'

Now it was my turn to laugh.

'A bit pretentious for a pack of cigarettes, no?'

Even in the near-dark I could see his eyes twinkle.

'We will soon be old friends,' he said.

He rose first, with difficulty. At his full height he was even more impressive – a bulky man whom age was withering from within. I mean that his body didn't fit his frame somehow. The mackintosh flapped on him like a cape.

'Can I assist you?' I asked.

'Yes, but not like that. I need to link my arm through *yours*.'

'Oh, I see.'

'And I don't, not very well, except out of the corners of my eyes. Ah yes, I see your youth now. Just to the duck pond will be fine. I like my quiet moments with the ducks.'

I half-expected him to march like an old soldier, but he had a stooped, languid gait. We ran out of things to say suddenly, and I looked at the moon.

'A waning moon,' I said eventually, as we neared the pond.

'Not full?'

'A sliver off.'

He stopped and swivelled round towards me, drawing up his whole bulk.

'Are you, then, *one of us*?'

I've been feeling the old restlessness stir in me again. *Now's not the time*, I tell myself. It's been good to have a life that's neatly parcelled out, to get up around the same time each day and go to bed around the same time each night. There is a point to softness after all.

Only, it doesn't hold me.

The restlessness starts at my feet and goes up my legs. I should lie on my back and kick my legs like a dying fly, buzz all the life out of me.

Why can't I get this old man out of my head?

I keep closing my eyes and hearing his voice. Like a voice I've heard somewhere before, or – crazy as it sounds – heard underwater. Yet when I try to recapture it, all I hear is a gruff monotone, except for that last boom. *One of us*. What did he mean? Why did I hurry away like that, leaving him laughing in pain, bent over as if to feed the ducks?

The next day I went back to the same spot. Well, I was curious about him. I'd collected Bibi after work, so it must have been around the same time. The weather was also the same – damp on the ground but no rain in the air, enough of a breeze to move some fallen leaves along, that's all. Nothing to deter him from setting out. How could he have lived here for so long unnoticed by me? Sat on a bench as if it belonged to him in a park I frequent almost daily, wearing a hat you won't see anywhere else in this ill-dressed city. Had I passed him as a girl? Maybe he'd called out to me fifteen years ago, as I skipped by. Or I'd called out to him. 'Mister, hey Mister. What you looking at, Mister?'

I got up and walked around and sat back down on his side of the bench. Even Bibi lay on the same spot, as if he understood. I wished I understood.

And now I remembered something else from the day before. As we'd walked towards the duck pond, a passer-by gave a slight bow in our direction. It was like we were suddenly living in a more chivalrous age, where gentlemen in parks bowed to gentleman-accompanied ladies. For one delirious moment it all seemed to fit: the hat, the linked arms, the slight bow, the mallard descending on the pond.

But the greeting wasn't for me. I saw that now. The slight bow was directed at the ailing man on my arm. Who was he?

If he wasn't in the park, he might be in his street. Transvaal Street, he'd said. Which was past my place. Bibi looked up at me. Poor dog, he gets more tired each day, now that we aren't couped up in that suffocating flat any more. 'I'll drop you off first, boy. Don't worry,' I told him.

Maybe night-time wasn't the right time to go looking. Or

maybe it was.

He should be living in an old farmhouse or a castle, not on this street that could be mistaken for any other street in the east. I walked quickly the whole length of it, and slowly back. Some people came in and out of various flats, not many, and all young. A boy dangled from a bar in the little play area, and a woman swept the pavement with an indoor brush. I looked in on a brown cafe, and on my way back I went inside. A coffee might help.

Gazing through scratched glass onto the street, I thought of the maze of streets I'd run through in my time here, when I had friends – a group of them, not always the same group – and the free run of what I took to be the world. We clustered together and we scattered, one of us darting out and the others following. I must have darted out more than most.

I took my empty cup to the counter.

'Another?' the barman asked. He had a dirty apron like a butcher's.

'No, thanks,' I said, adjusting myself on the stool. 'I was just looking for somebody who lives in this street. Unfortunately I don't have his house number. Maybe you know him. He's white-haired, tall, a bit frail. Sometimes he wears a black wide-brimmed hat, you know, like…'

'Who's asking?'

'Well, I am.'

He bristled at this.

'You want to know if I've seen an old bloke in a hat. This is a bar. I've seen a million old blokes in hats.'

'Not like this hat.'

'If it was the Pope's hat I still wouldn't say. You get me?'

'Maybe I'm his long-lost daughter. Maybe I've travelled halfway across the world to be here.'

'Then you'll know his house number.'

I hate to be the loser in a joust like this, especially when I walk away *admiring* the victor. So I dropped some coins for the coffee into my dirty cup.

Outside, the wind had whipped up, and I thought of the woman sweeping leaves into the gutter. Then I realised why: she was still sweeping – I could hear the sound of it from around the corner. She was an old woman. *Kin can be found among kin*, I thought, and walked towards the sound.

She was at the exact same spot, and I saw only now that she was more haggard than old. The brush ought to have been a broomstick to take her out of this world.

'Excuse me,' I said. 'Excuse me.'

On she went with her sweeping till the brush made contact with my foot. She looked up, her eyes a milky blue.

'Move your foot,' she said.

'I am looking for somebody. A man who wears a black coat and a black hat, this wide. He lives round here. He's lived here for the past twenty years.'

'Move your fucking foot.'

I moved my foot, and my whole body, out of her way.

I walked even more slowly now, to not seem intimidated. But I was intimidated, and I knew why: I am afraid of madness. That was also why I had hurried away from the man at the pond. Not that he was mad – the better I remembered him, the less mad he seemed – but his last words to me seemed mad, especially with that laugh again. I can't afford to be friendly with the mad, not in my situation of living hand to mouth – of being on the verge of living hand to mouth.

A postman walked towards me, then turned sharply, escaping into a lobby. I thought of waiting till he reappeared and repeating my question. And that's just what I did, engineering an ambush at the precise moment the door opened. Are postmen trained to be nonchalant? He brushed past me with a word I couldn't make out, leaving me the startled one.

Across the road the dangling boy was standing now. He smiled, as if he understood what had just happened. I crossed the road to interrogate him.

'Hello there. What's your name?' I asked, faking a smile.

'I don't speak to strangers.'

'Quite right. But I saw you smiling at me.'

'You keep walking up and down. It looks funny.'

'I bet it does. But, you know, the reason I'm doing that is because I'm worried about a man who lives in this street. I can't find him, and I need to find him. He wears a great big black hat. You must have seen him.'

He looked at my shoes, and then at my face. Then he looked at his own shoes.

'I can do the splits,' he said.

'Really? I'd love to see *that*.'

He spread his legs and fell over.

'See?'

'That's brilliant. You know the man I …'

'Uh-huh.'

He pointed to a spot behind me. I turned to where the woman was sweeping – where she wasn't sweeping.

There he was, hatless, passing the time of day with her, a madwoman with a brush, like he'd passed the time of day with me.

I turned back to the boy and thanked him. He shrugged his shoulders.

The man saw me before I reached him. I suppose I was approaching him from the side, and he could see sideways. If I was still smiling, he didn't mirror my expression. Had he forgotten me so soon?

There are moments when time itself seems to stop, even though we keep moving. My last few steps towards him were like that.

He leaned into the madwoman and said something she seemed to accept. She started sweeping again.

'Well, well, what have we here?' he said to me finally, not without warmth.

Despite all the time I had to prepare myself, I couldn't think what to say.

And then I could.

3

'I'm sorry I ran away.'

'Why would you not run away from me? A crazy man accosting you in a public park.'

'You're not crazy.'

'Since you seek reassurance… no, I am not.'

I glimpsed the red of the door at his back, asked, 'Is this where you live?', and he stepped aside. In the window a white plaster bust faced into the room.

'This is where I live.'

'I stood here at this spot looking for you. If I'd just looked in the window.'

'But we're here now. That's all that matters.'

'Were you going somewhere?'

'For my nightly libation. Do join me.'

'In that place? I'm afraid I insulted the barman just now.'

'Jan? No!'

'He wouldn't tell me where you live.'

'Yes, Jan is a fine fellow. What did you say to insult him?'

'It's not what I said. I left money for him in a dirty cup.'

'Well, that's not so bad, is it? Now take my arm. I'll lead –

you are on my patch now.'

And so he led, with evident pride, a smile on his grave face, tugging my arm needlessly as we crossed the road, so that I understood that he was not passively escorting me.

'I get the same small thrill approaching a bar as I did as a young man,' he said.

It was true that he seemed lighter of step suddenly. This got me wondering about him.

'Are you a heavy drinker?'

'The questions you ask!'

'It's just that I've known some people who are.'

When we got to the door, he opened it and tried to hold it open for me, but his arm barred my way. As I ducked underneath, he swivelled round to follow my movement and tripped. Jutting out my arm, I broke his fall to some extent, but his head still smacked off the ground. The barman Jan must have leapt over the bar, as he was beside us when I looked up.

'You again,' he said.

'Help me get him up,' I told him.

'No, no,' the old man said, waving his arms towards a lamp as if trying to beat back the light.

We set him on a chair, and he slumped in it with his legs spread out in front of him exactly like a man in a state of collapse. There was a cut on his head, and the blood was running thinly through his yellow hair – yellow and matted at that part of his head, perhaps from some kind of old-man's hair oil.

'That's a bad cut, Michiel,' Jan said. 'I should have something for it in the back.'

'No. Home!'

'Are you sure?'

'Home!'

'All right. I'll help you across the road.'

'No. *She!*'

For a moment, Jan looked at me without contempt.

'*She*'s not your …?'

'So long, Jan.'

Outside, he was steadier on his feet than I expected.

'So you're Michiel.'

'And you?'

'Femke.'

'Ah, a Friesian name. You really did rile Jan, didn't you?'

'I seem to have that effect on people.'

'People!'

I put the key in the red door for him, and the second key in his own door after that. I half-expected an old-person smell to waft towards me, but the smell of the place was almost fragrant.

It was a short hall – it was a small flat – and we could barely stand together in it, which we didn't do for long, as a sharp turn took us into the squarish living room. The suite there consisted of a two-seater wicker sofa and a wicker armchair, their back and seat cushions showing pallid roses on thorny stems. I should know because I arranged him first of all on the sofa, which he couldn't stretch out on comfortably, and then in the armchair, which left him tilting to one side like a drunk. He said he preferred the armchair and so I wedged a couple of cushions either side of him and sat down on the sofa with my hands clasped between my knees.

'Don't sit there so expectantly,' he said. 'Nothing will happen.'

'I'm trying to think what to do. You need that cut cleaned and covered. And you need a strong drink. Tell me where I can get what I need.'

'Well, the strong drink is on the bookshelf, right there.'

'Disinfectant, gauze?'

'Strong drink disinfects. As for gauze, you won't find anything like that here.'

'I'll go out and buy some.'

'Wait. Try the drawer next to the sink. I've seen a plaster or two there, now that I think of it.'

'What's this?' I asked, coming back from the kitchen with a red first-aid box in my hands. I had already opened it.

'It's a pretty box, isn't it? I got it in a flea-market. Don't think I ever looked inside.'

He didn't wince when I cleaned out his head-wound, merely babbled on in a sweet kind of way.

'The red cross is such a powerful emblem,' he was saying as I started to pay attention. 'They use a red crescent in Islamic states, you know. Understandable, given their experience of the Knights Templar during the Crusades. They say it isn't the cross of St George, but I like to think it is. The Redcrosse Knight from Spenser's *Faerie Queene*.'

He laughed at his own seriousness then. I poured a large drink into a cloudy tumbler. He drank it down two-handed, both hands trembling.

'This was Robert Louis Stevenson's favourite whisky,' he said. 'I approve of Stevenson, the author of *Jekyll and Hyde* and *Treasure Island* and a handful of first-rate poems.

Home is the sailor, home from the sea
And the hunter home from the hill.

That's marvellous, isn't it?'

'It'll be an education being around you. The trouble is,' I said, stopping his smile, 'I don't like to be educated.'

'A very good point, well made,' he said, raising his glass in my direction. I was back on the sofa, with my legs tucked under me, looking around the room and thinking that it wasn't unlike my own room – crowded and sparse at the same time. Too little room for the too few belongings.

'What do you do for entertainment? I mean, besides drinking and reading.'

'There is not much to my life now besides drinking and reading, and to speak truthfully my drinking days are behind me. My reading days too, given the state of these eyes. But I'll let you into a secret: I never found entertainment in either drink or books. No, never.'

'Then why bother?'

'To be entertained is to escape. I always wanted to find *a way in*. I expect this makes no sense to you.'

'It makes a kind of sense. My walks with Bibi are a bit like that. But I was only noticing the absence of a TV.'

'Oh, I have the radio for human company. That is very old-man of me, I know. But there you have it.'

I looked towards the mantelpiece that my eyes had swept over before.

'A Saba Freudenstadt, that one. The Germans know how to make radios.'

'Is it in working order?'

'Go ahead and try.'

'I'll take your word for it,' I said, and smiled. I was happy where I was, cradling my own glass in the space between the back of my thigh and my calf.

'The curious and the incurious are blended perfectly in you,' he said.

'I'll take that as a compliment.'

'As you should. But explain what you meant by that remark about walking your dog.'

'Do I have to?'

'Yes, because when the questioner is good-willed and has made a reasonable effort to understand yet remains puzzled, it is necessary to explain.'

'Seriously, you speak like this all the time?'

'Don't exhaust my patience, young woman.'

'What did I even say? It's such a struggle to have to think. You have your drink and your books and your radio. I have Bibi.'

'Then you win.'

This was altogether too sad for me to ignore, and so I got up and refilled his glass, inspecting first the radio and then his head in the process.

'I will tell you what I meant if you explain something to me too. All right?'

'All right.'

'A few years ago I grew afraid of the outside world, so my walks with Bibi were a way back into it. He was the cause of my terror, you could say – the reason I had to face the thing I feared. But he was also my comforter. I didn't fear the world half as much with him beside me. I grew less and less afraid and even started to enjoy our walks, but the terror was always there, ready to ambush me in a second. I have to steel myself, every time I attach the leash to his collar.'

'Where is your dog now?'

'My flatmate is taking care of him. I am pretending not to notice how close they're getting. Is that pathetic?'

'No, it's rather touching. Thank you.'

'What for?'

'For explaining.'

'So now it's your turn,' I said.

'Go right ahead.'

'That woman outside, with the brush. What is she to you?'

He said nothing at first. Then he said: 'What she is to me is a reminder not to exceed the stated dose.'

'That's not an explanation.'

'Yes, you're right,' he sighed. 'Her name is Mina. She's had a hard life. Some of the hardness of her life is down to me. I rejected her, you see, though I've always treated her kindly. She has battled several addictions: now, just the sweeping and I remain.'

'Doesn't it disturb you, that constant scraping?'

'Until you mentioned Mina, I hadn't noticed that she'd started up again. She will sweep like that until you leave. Off and on.'

'*Should* I leave?'

'It will be worse for her if you do. It's like your dog and this flatmate of yours. You saw something, a new alliance forming, and so you closed your eyes as you bowed to the inevitable. Poor Mina never learned to do that.'

4

He spoke lucidly like that for another twenty minutes before drifting off – a broad humpbacked clock, as ancient-looking as the German radio beside it, helped me keep track. I didn't know what to do, except that I knew not to leave him. I wasn't going to undress him, but I did fetch a quilt from the bedroom and drape it round him, tucking in his limbs as much as the quilt's folds. They always talk of accident victims spending a comfortable night in hospital: I wanted him to be comfortable, to get well, and (if I'm honest) to wake up feeling grateful.

When I took the quilt from his bed I tried not to look around me. This is a ridiculous hang-up from my life with Mother: the less I saw, the less she could accuse me of. Or no, she would still accuse, but I wouldn't look quite so guilty. Back in the living room, sitting opposite this now gently snoring man, I felt with a stab just how ridiculous I was being. Why shouldn't I look around? It wasn't like I was light-fingered.

I drew the line at going back to his bedroom though – he deserved some privacy – and I didn't open any drawers. I think this is the key to feeling virtuous: inventing rules where no one cares.

After a while I realised that the most interesting stuff was inside his books: tickets to the opera from years ago; ancient photographs, one of a high-sided pram with an angry-looking baby inside, another of a woman in a camel-hair coat, standing outside a pharmacist's; hand-written notes, the most intriguing of which said: 'Don't despair, not even over the fact that you don't despair. K.' That got me wondering. Who was K? A concerned colleague? His life's love?

Just the thought of the word 'colleague' sent me in a new direction. This man must have done something with his life, but what? Perhaps the radio was a clue. He seemed to know about such stuff. That could make him a collector, or even an engineer. But being a collector's not a profession, unless he ran an antiques shop – there are a few in the vicinity. And then he was the son of a diplomat – many sons follow in their father's footsteps. He is certainly well read, which could be an advantage in that line of work, where you need to be able to strike up a conversation with foreign strangers, just like Father had to do, though his line was business. Then again, all that reading made it more likely he was an academic of some sort: clearly he is used to being around young women. But I didn't want him to be some stuffy professor, and there were no signs of wealth that even bankrupt businessmen display, and he seemed too abrupt somehow to be a diplomat and too impatient to be able to sit in a draughty old antiques shop and much too wordy to be a simple engineer.

Despite my good intentions, I drifted back towards the

bedroom. It was thinking about Father that made me do it. I well remembered the pinstripe suits, the shirts and ties hanging in my parents' wardrobe. They could have left no one in doubt that here was a well-to-do businessman, precise and debonair. The wardrobe might be a revelation too.

One of the wardrobe doors lay invitingly open – well, the door catch wasn't quite caught – so I prodded it and it swung back by itself. No need for guilt there. That fragrant smell was even stronger inside the wardrobe, but it looked like there were no surprises in store, and no clues either. There were corduroy jackets and tweed jackets, with trousers underneath them that I didn't touch. The shirts were white or blue or pale yellow.

That would have been it, if my hand hadn't brushed against something that gave me goosebumps. To the side, behind the locked, mirrored part of the wardrobe, in a deeper dark than the rest, a plastic bin bag covered up whatever was hanging there. I manoeuvred it out into the light, lifted the wrinkled black plastic, and set it on the bed: a blue-and-white diamond-patterned dress. The diamonds were different shades of blue against the white. It looked old, but the sort of old a young woman could wear. I held it against me – I couldn't help myself – and thought, *A perfect fit!* In truth, it was a dress for an inch-taller woman. I rummaged some more, but it was the only dress there. What sort of memento was this? Whose?

I heard a snort from the living room and quickly covered up the dress again and put it back. Within seconds I was beside him, but it was all right, he was still snoring away, only with his head tilted awkwardly. Cupping his face with my hands, I moved his head so that it rested on the antimacassar once more, and the snoring subsided.

I went back to the bedroom to check my handiwork, to see that all was the same as before. It wasn't. The dress in its black covering had been hanging straight, but now a box jutted out from beneath, like a step up to it.

It was a cardboard box, unsealed, so of course this was another invitation. At the top of the box was a book, and under that the same book, and under that the same book again. So there was only need to take one into the light.

Collected Poems was the title. Then I saw the name, flipped the book over in my hands and saw the photo.

He looked all right, I must say. Middle-aged, so still too old for me even then. Which was when? I checked inside and saw that the year was 1984. Then I read the blurb. 'Michiel de Koning was born in Utrecht in 1930. In the first phase of his career he was closely associated with the elder poet Gerrit Achterberg. His most recent work, the mysterious, unsettling sequence *M*, divided the critics but proved a popular success on publication, despite appearing in English only, since the original version is (according to the author) "the property of its inspirer". The sequence can now be seen in its proper context: that of a lifetime's dedication to poetry.' And then some quotes, one in English about *M*: 'Each line is perfectly weighted, and weighed down with grief.'

None of this meant much to me, except that now I knew his full name, and that he was 72, or possibly 71, a poet, and an Utrechter. That could be something to rib him about, though I couldn't admit to knowing it yet.

Back in the living room I saw that he hadn't moved an inch. I thought that maybe I should leave, but a desire to see this through to the end, whatever the end was, made me stay. And, after all, he might have woken up confused. No, I couldn't leave. But as nurse I had certain rights, such as the right not to go hungry on the job. So I poured myself a glass of milk and made a sandwich with some Old Amsterdam cheese – the bread and cheese were both surprisingly fresh. The milk tasted odd after the whisky.

I tried to eat lying on the sofa, like a Roman, but I couldn't get comfortable. Instead I sat and looked at the man between each bite. Then I looked at the curtains, which were red, a deep wine-red, with pictures of birds stitched into them. The birds were kingfishers, and had an icy stare. I suppose all birds do. I liked working out the pattern and predicting which would come next, the bird perched or the bird swooping. Because it didn't simply alternate. Once I'd worked out the pattern, I knew exactly what the folds of the curtains hid. I liked the thought of those hidden birds.

My mind went back to the book. It had a green cover with white words – I might be able to find it on the shelves in this room. Or some other book of his. Well, authors are a vain lot.

But I was wrong, and glad to be wrong. Maybe this Michiel de Koning was not one of that lot. I took down the biggest book there was, a book of paintings by Vermeer, and found myself repeating what I'd just been doing, studying a curtain to work out what its pattern was, only in a book this time, and failing this time.

'You're spilling crumbs on the book.'

I nearly spat out the contents of my mouth.

'Christ! Will you not do that?'

'What?'

'Spook me like that.'

He was in the same position, but with his eyes open – open and bright, as if he'd been watching a while.

'Are you all right?' I said, forgetting about myself. I got up and went over to him and looked at his head.

'You had a nasty fall. Do you remember?'

'I remember… the Redcrosse Knight, you pouring me a drink. Where is my glass now?'

'It's on the stool beside you.'

'Would you?'

'I think we'll call it a night. It isn't good for your head.'

He seemed a bit crestfallen, asked sharply: 'Shouldn't you be getting back?'

'So you can pour yourself a drink when I'm gone? I don't think so.'

'I was thinking about your dog. Bibi. You see how well I remember now?'

'Bibi will be just fine. You, on the other hand …'

He shot me a piercing glance, which I reflected back at him. Then he seemed to sag a little, like a sail when the wind dies down.

'What did I do to deserve such an angel?'

'Nothing, and you don't.'

5

I stayed the night on the two-seater sofa, with his armchair pulled up alongside, so that I fell asleep with my body in an L-shape. He was fine after a light supper and one small drink that I allowed him. He accepted my presence, didn't even ask me to explain it, which was just as well. I wasn't ready to explain.

He was up before me, clattering about in the small toilet, and when I propped myself up on the arm of the sofa and looked around the door I saw him shaving – he'd left the toilet door wide open – with a blade, wearing a white dressing gown. His mirrored reflection said hello.

'Can I make you breakfast?'

'Only coffee first thing for me. But help yourself.'

I did help myself, and put his coffee on too. The aroma permeated the flat, nearly covering up the incense smell, which I commented on as he emerged dressed in fawn-coloured trousers and one of his pale yellow shirts.

'Not incense. That's the damp you smell,' he said.

He dropped into the armchair, and I fetched the coffee. I say 'fetched', but I didn't feel like a servant – or worse.

'*Two* sugars?'

'Old men are full of surprises,' he said.

'Not always.'

'You know some who aren't?'

'I mean old men aren't always full of surprises. You aren't all that old, you know. You are sitting in the same chair you sat on yesterday.'

'And you on the same sofa.'

'Because you sat on the chair first.'

'So it goes.'

'What does that even mean?'

I was softening towards him. He was about to eat the piece of cake I'd cut for him against orders, and I had to look away because his hand was trembling so badly.

'Another Dutch girl who likes it plain as day.'

'A Dutch girl who's had enough enigma in her life.'

'At the hands of men?'

'Are you implying there were many? Well, there were some, but you are so maddening. It always has to be about you.'

'One man in particular?'

I looked at his hands, which were steadier now, and picked a tiny feather out of the cushion's stuffing, blew on it, and placed it against my lips. I don't know how long the moment lasted. When I looked up, Michiel was standing over me.

'Are you all right?'

'Yes. I was just…'

'I'm sorry, I shouldn't have probed like that. Your life is none of my business.'

'But I want it to be.'

He smiled at that, a kindly smile. He was the one assisting *me* now, taking the cushion out of my hands, and replacing it with my mug. It was a white mug, with a design of blueberries on it.

'Finish your coffee,' he said. 'Before it gets cold.'

'You were right,' I said, setting the mug back down. 'There was someone in particular. I hadn't thought about him in a while.'

'You don't have to explain.'

'He was a lot like you. An artist.'

'I am an artist? Who said so?'

'I don't know. The barman, maybe. You *are* some kind of artist, aren't you?'

'I don't regard poetry as an art. More an illness.'

'*He* thought of himself as a poet too, but in a different medium. I remember him saying that.'

'And you were his Muse.'

'I never thought that. Maybe he did.'

'When did he leave you?'

'Well, now. Who left who is a… No, you're right. I did the staying, he did the leaving.'

'When?'

'I don't know when. I thought we were still together when

we weren't. Then when I found out we weren't, I did something to bring it all to a head. The last I heard of him he was in Pieter Lastman Quay. I expect he is back in England now.'

'Ah, an Englishman.'

'There you go again.'

'What did I say?'

'Nothing. But you make it sound like something.'

'Sorry. I said "Ah" because the picture's clearer. It becomes clearer with every detail. No detail's too small.'

'If you want the story of my life, you'll be waiting a long time,' I said. 'There's no story.'

'There are only stories. But I don't have a long time, and I was never patient.'

'What about you? Who's your lost love?'

I said that with so much warmth that the dark look he flashed at me really penetrated, all the way to my bones. Now it was my turn to say sorry. And I would have, if a key hadn't turned in the door.

'Only me.'

In came a woman wearing a beige coat and carrying a large black bag. She stopped when she saw me.

'Oh, hello. We have company today.'

'This isn't your day for coming round, Martina,' Michiel said to her.

'Tomorrow is my niece's wedding, remember.' She spoke loudly for no apparent reason.

'Martina, this is Femke.'

'Hello, Femke,' she said briskly. 'I am the community nurse. What happened to your head?'

'He fell,' I said.

'I was asking Mr De Koning, dear.'

'I fell.'

I smiled at that. Already it felt like we were conspirators.

'Why do you have a key?' I asked, as she looked through her bag without answering.

'This needs a good clean. The bruising is quite specific. Did you land on something sharp?'

'No, just my head,' he said.

'You might have struck the corner of the table as you fell,' I said. 'I never noticed.'

'Which table?' she asked, looking around.

'In the brown cafe. What's it called?'

She looked at him as a mother looks at a naughty child. Not a good mother. He had stayed silent throughout.

'You managed to get out of the house, then. So you can do that now?'

'I helped him,' I said.

'I'm sure you did. Can you bring me a bowl of warm water from the kitchen, dear?'

In the kitchen, waiting for the kettle to warm up, I had a look through the cupboards, listening the whole time. If he answered her questions, it must have been in a whisper. I couldn't make sense of her anger.

There was a set of four Chinese bowls I liked the look of. Other than that, nothing remarkable. I found a broad shallow bowl and half-filled it with the half-boiled water.

I thought she needed the water for him, but she dipped her hands in it – there was some kind of gel on them, I noticed – then dried them with a stretch of blue paper towel. She really did seem to be some kind of a nurse.

'Are you a friend of Mr De Koning?' she asked when we were alone. Michiel had gone into the bedroom 'to prepare himself', I didn't know for what.

'We only just met, but yes, I think so.'

'That's nice. Are you writing a thesis about him?'

'A thesis?'

'So you're not a student?'

'No.'

'He does still get the odd letter from young people studying his work.'

'You get to see his letters?'

'My dear, you seem to have a very narrow idea of the work I do. In many respects I am Mr De Koning's eyes and ears.'

'He has his own eyes and ears. Why don't you want him to leave his flat?'

'It isn't a matter of not wanting him to leave. He can't. Or he couldn't. If he is not in fact housebound, I can't possibly justify the number of visits I make. It's about the hours, you see.'

'But he fell. It wasn't a very successful outing.'

'That's true. I'll be sure to mention that. I see you are a good friend, after all.'

'Do you masturbate the old man?'

Well, there had to be some comeback for that 'after all'. She stiffened and went white. Then she started shouting.

'Mr De Koning! Mr De Koning!'

Michiel staggered out of the bedroom, his trousers slipping down.

'I must insist that this young woman leave immediately.'

'Why? What's she done?'

'I must *insist*.'

'I really can't…'

'Then *I* will be forced to leave.'

'But I haven't had my injection yet.'

'It's all right, Michiel,' I said, placing my hand over his, which was trembling again. 'I'll come back later.'

'That's settled, then,' she said.

Michiel looked lost for a moment.

'Thank you for your attentions, Martina. They are at an end now.'

'But that's impossible. Mr De Koning, you are being… hasty.'

'Yes, I am like that.'

'Very well,' she said, holding back what seemed like tears – holding them well back. I almost felt sorry for her. 'I will arrange for a colleague to visit you.'

She tried to leave then, but Michiel barred her exit with his arm.

'I wish the very best for your niece, Martina. Tell her that.'

'I will.'

'I would like you to return the key now.'

6

After the door clicked shut – she didn't slam it, at least – we stood facing each other, he with his trousers round his ankles, shaking like a leaf, yet somehow, too, as strong as a tower. Now as I say it I picture the Weeper's Tower, the one Henry Hudson left from on his way to discovering Manhattan, as every schoolchild learns. The last time I passed it there was a life-sized model elephant on the terrace. Such is life in the city.

'Let me,' I said, buttoning his trousers. No, not a button, it was one of those metal fasteners that slide into place. It was only when it did that I realised I should be feeling awkward. He looked awkward, or maybe quizzical.

'You didn't shave very cleanly,' I said.

As he rubbed his chin, I turned on my heels and headed straight for his chair.

'So you're housebound. How come I met you by yourself in the park the other day?'

'Interrogations should be done by spotlight, not daylight.'

'Sit down and answer me.'

He laughed at that, though I didn't mean to be funny. Then he sat on the sofa, where I had sat.

'You met me on a good day, if I dare call it that. I have good days when I make it as far as the park, oh, about once a year.'

'And your visits to the bar?'

'Yes, well, they are a more regular occurrence, it's true to say. What annoyed Martina, *really*, wasn't my going there so much as my drinking once I'd got there. I was rather flustered when she arrived just then. Didn't give me time to hide *that*, or *those*.'

He was pointing to the bottle of whisky and the two whisky glasses.

'I'll clear those up,' I said, taking the two glasses and putting them on the shelf. I removed a book and put it back with the bottle behind it. Then I took the glasses through to the kitchen.

'That do?' I asked as I passed.

'Such subterfuge', he called through, 'is really no longer necessary.'

'Martina's replacement will call one day. I can't have you getting into trouble again.'

'There won't be any replacement.'

'How come?' I asked, back in the room now.

'She knows as well as I do that I am not entitled to the care she provided for me.'

'What about the injections?'

'Those…' he said, with a wave of his hand.

'What are they? Insulin?'

'No. A form of amphetamine.'

'You're not serious.'

'I'm afraid I am.'

'That can't be legal.'

'No, and I haven't told you. Not for my sake – Martina's.'

'What a dark horse she is. And you. But why's she so concerned about your drinking, then?'

'It's unfathomable, isn't it? This Lutheran conscience of ours, accepting window-whores but not poor punctuality.'

'Window-whores? You really *are* old-fashioned. And you should know I was brought up a Catholic.'

He gave me a long and searching look, but said nothing. I said nothing back. After a while, I gave up.

'Well, what do we do now?'

'I'll tell you,' he said, suddenly animated. (I noticed early on how he would come to life suddenly, as a result of something said, and then just as suddenly droop, also as a result of something said. Words were so important around him.) 'Now that I have use of my legs again, why don't you show me your world?'

'If you like. But you always had use of your legs,' I said, fake-defiant, helping him out of the sofa.

In the street, he asked me about Bibi. I said we could see him now. Why not? I wasn't too worried about the state I'd left the place in. Now that I was a good citizen, working for the bread on my table, I liked to keep my life neat, which meant putting my clothes away in the drawers for putting clothes in, and not leaving the duvet in a heap, and wiping the few surfaces there were.

But as I turned the corner into my street, my heart began to thud, and I felt glad of his arm that was threaded through mine.

'You are trembling,' he noticed.

'Hush.'

I let us in, and was struck by how bare the place seemed, as if I was back from holiday as a child. It had only been one night. A day and a night.

I led him to a wooden chair in the kitchen, put on the kettle, and went off to my room to fetch Bibi. He wasn't there. I knocked on my flatmate Bart's door. When he opened it, I quickly saw that Michiel was at my back.

'Oh, it's you,' Bart said. 'Is this your father?'

Bibi was already licking the palm of my hand. Michiel stepped forward and patted him too.

'A fine dog,' he said. 'Really a very fine dog.'

'You should say if you're going to be away all night,' Bart said. 'I had to buy food for him, there was nothing in your cupboard.'

'I am Michiel,' Michiel said. 'There is no need to scold. I took a bad turn and Femke looked after me. It is good that you were here to take care of the dog.'

'How much did you spend on his food?' I asked. 'I can repay you.'

'Join us in the kitchen,' Michiel said. 'We were about to have tea. That's right, isn't it?'

I smiled at how delicately Michiel put everything. Bart was like putty in his hands. To be fair, Bart was like putty in my hands too.

We drank tea under a large wine-dark sheet that was spread over the pulley. Michiel kept on looking at us while he sipped his tea – I hadn't noticed before how watchful he could be.

'You have a nice room, Bart,' he said.

'The coffin,' Bart joked, then looked embarrassed, as if he shouldn't say 'coffin' to Michiel.

'I always liked small rooms,' Michiel said. 'Large rooms make me feel diminished. As if I've stepped into a large field with too much sky overhead. My ancestors must have lived in narrow caves.'

'Where are Kaat and Pim?' I asked, embarrassed myself now. I had staked a lot on Michiel not being a crazy man.

'Walking the dogs.'

'They never think to take Bibi too?' Michiel asked.

'Bibi won't walk with other dogs,' I said, as Bart left the room. After a few seconds, I heard the door of the hall toilet close. I put the kettle on again.

'Is that so?' Michiel asked.

'Yes. He's a loner, like his owner,' I said, smiling. 'Though, technically, I don't own him.'

'Who does?'

'My aunt Ceciel. She pays the dog tax. Officially, Bibi lives with her.'

'And where's that?'

'Up near the Hilton. I never go there.'

'Don't you like your aunt?'

'She dispenses a lot of advice. I don't like to be advised.'

'I'd like to meet her.'

'Well, you can't.'

'Let's go there now.'

'Absolutely not.'

'Aunt Ceciel,' I said, loud enough to be overheard. 'I have a friend who would like to meet you. The poet Michiel de Koning.'

There was a long silence, from a house of long silences.

'Is this another one of your stories?'

'We can come round now, if you like.'

'Not now, not now. I must…'

'Tomorrow, then? For *afternoon tea*. He will like that.' Aunt Ceciel could never resist putting on an afternoon tea.

'Yes, I suppose…'

'We'll see you then.'

'Wait. Femke. You and this – poet. Are you…'

'Friends. Yes, we are. He must be about your age, Aunt Ceciel. Judging by.'

'Tell him he is very welcome.'

'You are very welcome at Jan van Goyen Quay tomorrow, Michiel. Number 7.'

'He's there now? Femke, *really*.'

'Bye, Aunt Ceciel.'

I went back to bask in the look of delight on Michiel's face, but he looked suddenly drawn, ashen.

'You all right?'

'Yes,' he smiled weakly. 'So, tomorrow with your aunt. How is she related to you?'

'My mother's sister.'

'I see.'

'Though you couldn't find two sisters less alike. She has the most English Dutch accent you've ever heard. Has a picture of the English queen on her wall, alongside Beatrix and Juliana.'

Bart came back in, blushing slightly. I felt like saying, *You've been an age in that toilet*, just to deepen the blush. But all I said was: 'Your tea will be cold. Do you want another cup?'

'Please,' he said.

I listened, over the kettle's build-up, to their discussion of plants – Bart was studying botany. The subject seemed to revive Michiel, and I happily busied myself with my back turned to them. Actually I was inspecting a teaspoon, the ridiculous windmill sails at the handle-end. There would be nothing so trashy at Aunt Ceciel's.

7

'You had a phone call this morning. From Mohammed?'

We already had our coats on, were already on the way to my workplace – Michiel had asked to see it – when Bart remembered to tell me.

'Did he say what he wanted?'

'He mentioned you working an extra shift.'

'When?'

'This morning.'

'I don't mean when did he call.'

'Neither do I.'

Michiel put his arm in mine.

'You could have told me before now.'

'Sorry.'

It wasn't very far, but I couldn't walk as quickly as I wanted, and I think Michiel knew this, as he more than matched my step – not a clever thing to do when we were joined together. We were halfway to the offices before I realised that I could have called first. Panic is like that.

'It's all right,' he said again.

'It's all right for you,' I said, harshly – I never believe people when they're being reassuring. 'But this job is all I've got.'

'Come, come.'

I almost threw his arm off me. But we were approaching the door.

'I'll wait here,' he said, leaning against another door to the side – an entrance to what was left of the old burnt church. It was still blocked off.

'All right,' I said, softening at the sight of his breathlessness – which he was about to make worse by lighting a cigarette. I held the lighter steady for him. 'I might have to work straight away, but I'll come and tell you first.'

Inside, it wasn't hard to see why Mohammed had called. There must have been some kind of party here – odd for so staid a place. I didn't have time to look, but I looked anyway. A sad sort of a party. Purple streamers. Crushed plastic tumblers. Cake crumbs.

He was in the first-floor broom cupboard, reaching for something that was just out of reach. I startled him, which isn't a good thing to do to a man, any man, least of all a man of Mohammed's temperament.

'What do you want?'

'You wanted me.'

'Well I don't want you now.'

'I didn't get your message till now.'

'You're too late.'

'No I'm not. I'll make a start in the lobby. Was there some kind of …'

That was another bad move. He swivelled round and nearly knocked my jaw out of its socket – accidentally, but there was no apology.

'You're too late. I have an agency girl to help me. Her fee would come out of your earnings if you hadn't just been paid. Now go. I need someone reliable.'

'Mohammed, you can't.'

I heard breathing at my back.

Michiel!

'Mohammed, this is Michiel de Koning.'

They nodded to each other.

'Mohammed here is firing me, for not being in when he phoned.'

I waited for Michiel to speak.

'Excuse me,' Mohammed said.

Michiel moved aside as Mohammed walked away, bottles of blue cleaning fluid in his arms. Mechanically I switched the cupboard light off.

'I'm done here,' I said, actually biting my lower lip. I know that because a second later I tasted blood.

'Come here,' Michiel said, putting his arm around me at last. 'Let me treat you to a coffee. There's a cart outside.'

'Do you remember when this was a church?' I asked him.

'Naturally! And you?'

'Yes. I hated it. So gloomy.'

'You can't have been knee-high then.'

'I can remember this place from when I was in my pram. All of it.'

'How extraordinary. They say that geniuses can remember further back than the rest of us. Perhaps you're one.'

'And not you?'

'In the original sense of the word, a genius was a guardian spirit, you know.'

'No, I didn't know. You weren't much of a guardian spirit *in there*.'

That silenced him. But in the silence I panicked.

'We left without Bibi!'

'Don't worry, we can go back now and get him. It's good he didn't witness your distress.'

'Was I so bad?'

'Not so bad.'

'Let's cross to the other side, you should never turn back on yourself.'

'So people say. I don't know any other way to turn.'

But we did cross over, after Michiel took fright at a gang of kids. I began to realise just how frail he was, in some ways. I thought he had lied about going to the park only once a year, but it seemed to be true. So it was heroic, I suppose, that he had come this distance with me. No wonder he couldn't stand to be alone outside the offices.

He would walk a few yards, stop and sip his coffee with

trembling hands (both hands), then make a start again. The wind was whipping up. I had to wheel him round as he was about to step onto the tram track, just as the Number 19 drew up. He thanked me for that, like a man tipping his hat. He was from another time, maybe even another planet.

'I wouldn't go so far,' he said, startling me.

'What?'

'I wouldn't normally go so far without my cane.'

'You have a cane?'

'Yes.'

'But I haven't seen you with it.'

'No.'

'Why is that?'

'Oh, I don't know. It isn't nice being old with the young. One wants to be young oneself.'

I was touched by this confession.

'You'll be hiding your reading glasses next.'

'No, they can't help me now.'

'So you never read?'

'Not any more. Martina used to read to me.'

'Some nurse she was!'

'Yes.'

'And now I've chased her away. I could read to you.'

'Would you?'

I knew very well he was angling for me to say so. And I knew he knew I did. As long as any manipulation is out in the open, I don't mind it.

Now it was my turn.

'I'm looking forward to you meeting Aunt Ceciel. I'm such a disappointment to her, she'll be pleased to know I keep such… distinguished company.'

'I'll be on my best behaviour, don't worry.'

'So let's see this cane, then,' I said when we arrived at my place. We were just in the door, still with our coats on, and I wanted to get going. I was fixing the leash to Bibi's collar when Michiel said, 'Actually, Femke, I am a little tired.'

'I'm sorry. I'll make us some tea first.'

'No, I mean, I had better be getting back now.'

'I get it. Time's up.'

'It's just that I need to rest.'

'And you need to be alone for that.'

'Age doesn't come alone.'

This wasn't the first time he had said that. I couldn't tell if he was an old man repeating himself or if he regarded this saying as his mantra.

'Stop playing the age card. It's all right, I know how tiring I can be. Plenty have said.'

'I never tire of you, my dear. Never.'

'You've only known me five minutes.'

'An exhilarating five minutes, though. And now I must rest.'

'Let us walk you to the corner, at least.'

'Absolutely.'

Bibi kept straying towards Michiel, almost tripping him up. I considered this a good sign.

'I still want to see that cane of yours.'

'It's there, it's there. Next time you call you'll see.'

'That will be tomorrow. Remember? Aunt Ceciel?'

'Oh, yes.'

'She'll expect us at four. I'll call round after three. The 14 tram will take us there.'

'So many numbers.'

I thought of that when I turned up at his flat the next day, pressing the buzzer again and again, and knocking on the windows. Nothing. Had I confused him with my talk? Then I started to wonder if he wasn't there after all. He wouldn't have to lie behind the sofa or under the bed – the kitchen and hall were both screened from view. But why would he do that? Then I worried that he was there, but ill, lying unconscious or in agony. I looked and listened harder. Nothing again.

Then I got it – got him. He had heard everything – Aunt Ceciel's address, the time she expected us. Give him a finger, and he will take the whole hand: he was that kind of man. So he had gone before me. Met the old lady on his own terms. And I would arrive to find the old ones already conspiring, greeting me as if *I* was the stranger. That was all right – it was a pleasant trap to fall into.

Wine wouldn't be right, so I bought a slab of butter cake from the all-day night shop, holding it carefully in my lap on the tram. Aunt Ceciel would turn up her nose, but not as much as she would if I arrived empty-handed. I didn't have the money for the sort of thing that pleases her. Wouldn't have arranged to meet at all if I'd known my job was to be taken from me. It would be the first thing she'd ask about. Oh God. If Michiel said anything...

That bourgeois street. I walked its length till I felt my skin smoulder from the burning stares – not that I saw any – and turned into Aunt Ceciel's path without hesitating. Four steps, four raps on the door, and one step back. Her unmistakable shape forming in the frosted glass.

'Where is your gentleman friend?' she asked, looking out as I stepped inside.

8

For a woman who had always contrived to look like an old lady, Aunt Ceciel was mercifully free from old-lady odours. As I entered her hallway, I thought of the stale, biscuity smell in the flat I'd lived in before. Nothing like that here. Everything was spick and span, and smelled like it. Aunt Ceciel led me into the sitting room, not a hair in her swirly silver bun out of place.

My heart sank when I saw the spread she had laid out.

'You've gone to so much trouble, Aunt Ceciel, but I'm afraid Michiel may not be able to make it after all.'

'Why ever not?'

'I wish I knew. He was so keen to come. I called on him but he wasn't there. I'm a bit worried, to tell you the truth.'

'Oh, you needn't be. He was always flighty, that one.'

'You *know* him?'

If a body can collapse yet still convey strength, I'd say she collapsed into her chair. I know I collapsed into mine, but weakly.

'Yes, yes, in our younger days. Mieke more so.'

'He knew Mother?'

'He knew us both. I was more his age than Mieke was. You

can ask her about him yourself.'

'You know we don't speak.'

'This may be a means of breaking the ice.'

'No. I feel… betrayed.'

'By your mother?'

'Michiel.'

'Oh, he may not have put two and two together.'

'Or maybe he did. Maybe that's why he isn't here.'

We sat in stupefied silence, till she said: 'We may as well tuck in.'

I say things against myself, but one good thing about me – if it *is* good – is that I don't take on the colour of my surroundings. But with Aunt Ceciel I make an exception, always, and without ever meaning to. So it was I found myself biting delicately into the delicate sandwiches and attempting to speak properly – in proper sentences that made sense, not choked off half-way-through. But I felt choked, and as if on the verge of an awful discovery. Just how intimately had Mother known Michiel? I couldn't broach the subject *this* far with Aunt Ceciel. I would find out from the man himself. That's if I could keep my hands from wringing his neck first.

'How is your new job?'

Here we go. Nice of her, at least, to call it a new job, as if there had ever been an old one.

'It's just some cleaning work.'

'I told you you could do it. You can achieve anything you

set your mind to, Femke, I've always been very clear about that. The trouble with you has always been your reluctance to set your mind to anything that is the equal of your talents.'

'So you are ashamed of my cleaning job, then?'

'Not at all. Every ladder has a first rung. What about your poet friend? Might he have some work for you to do?'

'I hadn't thought of that,' I said, thinking about it now for the first time.

'These fellows aren't always the most organised of people. Somebody has to pop their masterpieces in the post.'

'You sound as if you knew a writer once.'

'Nicolaas had writers at the bank. Financial writers, not quite the same, but still… Poor Nicolaas had to hold their hands a good deal of the time.'

'I forget you had a husband,' I said, thoughtlessly. I shouldn't have said it out loud.

'Do you? Of course you were just a baby when Nicolaas was in his prime. And then his health failed, and we were away in the country for the best part of the year. I hardly saw you or your mother then.'

'But I remember coming here. Going all the way up into the attic rooms while you and Mother talked down here.'

'That would have been after Nicolaas passed away. I wonder what you did up there. There were never any toys in the house for you to play with.'

'I used to polish the shoes that were lined up in a rack. Not with polish. I'd rub them with my dress.'

At that, tears flowed. I barely noticed at first – she had bowed her head, even continued to nibble away at her sandwich – but soon I was holding her in my arms, as I had never done.

'For some reason I could never part with his shoes,' she said, when she was able to speak again. 'I couldn't bear to look at them, which is why they ended up at the top of the house. He would polish them until he could see his face in them, every evening. That was something he always did for himself. Of course, I insisted he place a newspaper underneath. He insisted on using de Volkskrant, which was my paper. "A Catholic rag," he called it. We never did see eye to eye on religion.'

She took my arms and moved them back towards my body, so that my hands ended up folded together on my lap. This was such an Aunt Ceciel pose that I laughed.

'That's the spirit,' she said. 'What about a game of Rummikub?'

'All right,' I said, and she fetched the box from the sideboard.

'Be a dear and take the dishes into the kitchen. But leave the nut bowl. And bring the jug of iced tea from the fridge and two tall glasses.'

She placed the numbered tiles into a bag and shook them. We used to do it differently at home: Mother would have spread out the tiles face-down on the table. No two sisters were ever less like each other. I mentioned this.

'We were known as the Apple and Pear Sisters,' she said. 'You might mention that to Michiel. It may ring a bell.'

'I wonder if he would be any good at Rummikub,' I said, more to myself.

'I shouldn't think so, though you never know. Sometimes these word men are good at other things too. But mostly not.'

There was such a twinkle in her eyes, which were still gleaming from her tears, that I wanted to throw my arms around her immediately. This wasn't the staid aunt I'd known and almost feared. How wrong you can be about somebody. I can be.

'You draw first.'

I did, and drew 13.

'No competing with that,' she said. 'You start.'

If I had the upper hand in the game at that point, it was the last time I would have it. I saw yet another side of Aunt Ceciel as she trounced me and took delight in doing so. Of course, we were keeping everything light, after the revelation about Michiel and the story of the shoes. I expect I will have to wait till dementia sets in with her before I really learn anything about the past. Today was like a short-lived storm in the middle of a drought. In the middle of a desert. To think of how all those people I knew from the squat – how long ago *that* seemed now – would spill themselves out, tell their life story to stoned or indifferent ears. *I* had listened, but only like a cat listens when you put food down for it. To make sure nobody was going to interfere with me.

I felt like overstaying my welcome, but I could see how tired she was getting. People always get tired after tears. I washed up and put everything away – in the wrong places, I'm sure – while Aunt sat with her feet up on a pouffe and watched TV. I had never known it to be on, not even when I came here as a child. I suppose some of her strictness was slipping away with age. Everyone is the same as everyone else deep down.

I looked in on her before I left. Of course she had some parting words of wisdom.

'My dear, be careful,' she said. 'You have come so far in the past year. Don't let any man – not even the great Michiel de Koning – set back your progress now.'

I insisted on seeing myself out, and surprisingly she let me. A shiny black Mercedes-Benz pulled up next door just as I stepped outside. The tinted windows made me curious, but not much. Then a man got out on the road side and darted round to open the pavement-side rear door. I knew right away the face that emerged, though the name didn't instantly register in my mind.

Then it did. 'Margriet,' I said, as the princess looked at me and glanced over my shoulder. I swear she smiled approvingly before making a regal beeline for Number 5's red door. The approval wasn't of me, I suddenly thought, but of the house I'd left. Just how well-connected *was* Aunt Ceciel?

The door-opener and another slick bruiser in shades – security, obviously – followed her in. The one in shades had the gall to turn to me and hiss: 'You say "Madam" or you say nothing.'

9

I was in two minds about what to do. Go back to the flat or go straight to Michiel's and – if he happened to be there – have it out with him. Have what out, though? That he might vaguely or less vaguely have known Mother and my aunt? Thinking it through, Michiel was 72, possibly 71, and Aunt Ceciel wasn't quite the old lady she made out to be. She was a good ten years older than Mother – as Mother never tired of pointing out – and Mother was in her early thirties when she had me. So Aunt Ceciel must be in her 60s now. Not exactly contemporaries, but in this district they might well have known one another. The sisters knew *him*, but then it seemed he was a celebrity of sorts. Not so that his name was ever bandied about in our house. It was a house almost without books once Father was gone. Only his encyclopaedias remained.

But, then, if Michiel did know who I was – whose daughter I was – and had kept quiet about it, that was a kind of betrayal. And I can't stand to be betrayed. At least, I couldn't that one time. Well, who can? But with me it's ridiculous. It isn't as if I've led a blameless life, either.

Suddenly I was a detective, going over every possibility

in my head, making connections that were weird and some not so weird – such as thinking of Uncle Nicolaas's shoes and noticing in memory that Michiel had a small shoe rack just beside his front door, with only one pair of shoes on it. Soft, brown shoes, not quite what you'd expect. But wasn't there also a pair of hard, black shoes in that wardrobe – the one with the diamond-patterned dress in it? I hadn't thought of that dress in a while. Or else I was always thinking of it – it's hard to tell the difference sometimes.

I got off the tram at the museum stop and walked through the park. Odd to do that without Bibi beside me, and I caught myself more than once looking down at my feet. I knew where I was headed, without letting the thought form in my head. And so I ended up at the bench where I'd first met Michiel as if it was a surprise. It might've been a good place to let my swarming thoughts settle, except that it wasn't.

Transvaal Street next. It was getting dark, so I could see as I approached his flat that a light was on. He'd better have a good explanation.

Three heads. The bust of Blake in the window, Michiel's, and another man's.

It was the stranger who opened the door to me, saying, 'Hello, you must be Femke.'

I made a beeline for Michiel.

'Aunt Ceciel sends her regards. Apparently you are old friends. Or was that my mother?'

'Femke, Femke,' he said wearily, a trembling hand brushing his forehead.

'Can I have a word?' the stranger said.

I stepped into the hall and then the kitchen with this other man.

'My name is Paul Vandervoort. I am an old writer-friend of Michiel's. I called this morning and found Michiel in a very bad way. We are just back from the hospital.'

'The hospital?'

'Yes. They wanted to carry out some tests, but Michiel refused to stay the night there. I couldn't talk him out of it, and of course we can't compel him to. He does seem to have perked up.'

'I won't have it. I won't be talked about in another room.'

He was in the doorway, leaning on the door frame. Not in a strong way. Not like some old-time movie star.

'I'm sorry, Michiel,' Paul said. 'You are quite right.'

'Femke, I didn't know,' Michiel said, supporting himself on my arm now, with a surprisingly tight grip. 'Not until your phone call with your aunt. Then it dawned on me.'

'What did?' I asked. I suppose I should have been more conciliatory, but too much was at stake.

'That you are the Pear Sister's daughter.'

'So Mother was the Pear?'

'And Ceciel the Apple. Yes.'

'What on earth?'

We both turned towards the bemused friend. It was a moment of lightness, at last.

The conversation continued in the living room – by fits and starts, with Michiel struggling at times for breath, or possibly to remember. But he did remember. Some kind of sophisticated bohemian scene in the neighbourhood, with its teenage and non-teenage hangers-on.

'I was *nel mezzo del camin di nostra vita*,' Michiel said.

'He means he was thirty-five,' Paul explained.

'And your mother could only have been in her mid-teens. She was a striking beauty. Ceciel less so. But Ceciel was hardly there at all, except to keep an eye on your mother. Ceciel had a proper job, unlike most of us.'

'Weren't you lecturing then?' Paul asked.

'Yes, but it was a time of turmoil. Only two or three years before the protests of '68. And I sided with the students, you see.'

'I remember it well.'

'Well, I don't,' I said. Now it was my turn to have amused heads turn towards me.

'Quite. It was all a long time ago, nearly as long as yesterday,' Michiel said.

'I don't understand that.'

'When you are my age, you will.'

I was getting somewhere, but not where I wanted to be – Michiel's closeness to Mother.

'Perhaps we should leave this discussion for another time,'

Paul said, clearly worried about Michiel's health.

'I think not,' I said, and Michiel gave a consenting glance.

'You mustn't think there was anything... untoward,' he said. 'They were very much on the periphery. Or I was on their periphery. Anyhow, I hardly knew them.'

'Yet you recall their nicknames half a lifetime later.'

'That's astute. I hardly *knew* them, or they me. But they made an impression. And I feed on impressions. Always did.'

'I never had you marked down as an *Impressionist*, Michiel,' Paul said, too obviously changing the subject.

'Isn't that how old Thomas Hardy described himself? The greatest English poet after Shakespeare and Blake. Who am I to differ?'

'You and the *English*,' Paul said. They were taking the talk in a direction I couldn't follow.

'And what impression was that?' I asked. 'Other than that the two were unlike?'

'I don't know that they were. Those were the names people gave them. Amusing names, but probably wide of the mark.'

'Not very.'

'Ah, so. I think beauty made your mother different. Different to us men, who behave like babies around beauty.'

'Did you behave like a baby?'

'Not as a result of your mother, no.'

That 'not' and that 'no' meant all to me. I could finally breathe.

'We must let Michiel rest. I insist on it,' Paul said again. This time I had no objection.

We laid him out on the bed, fully clothed but with his shoes off – those brown, soft shoes. It astonished me that he let us, but he did seem supremely tired. Perhaps this raking over the distant past really was exhausting him. And now I was left with the other white-haired man, who showed no signs of wanting to leave.

'How do you two know each other?' Either of us could have asked this, but I had got in first.

'Some silly people say we were part of the same school of poets. Can you imagine Michiel in any kind of *school*?'

'Not really, no.'

'I suppose I might have been. The school of Achterberg, they named it. After Gerrit Achterberg. Did you ever hear of him?'

'Yes. On the cover of Michiel's book.'

'His *Collected*?'

'That's right. But don't say. I found it by accident when I was cleaning up.'

'Oh dear. That was the cause of a falling out between us. You see, I wrote the blurb. It infuriated Michiel.'

'Why?'

'First of all because I drew attention to the link with Achterberg. Michiel had long since fallen out with *him*. Though never, in fact, repudiated him, which is interesting.'

I mustn't have looked very interested, judging by the glance he gave me.

'And secondly, because I made so much of "*M*", how it was such a mystery. That provoked his ire. *You have set the blood hounds loose*, he said to me.'

'What does that mean? And what is so mysterious?'

'More to the point, *who* is?'

'Well?'

'If we knew that, dear, perhaps we really could restore Michiel to health. She was his great love. His last – and, I believe, only – great love.'

10

'Gerrit Achterberg was a murderer.'

Paul was by now puffing on his pipe. I grew up in a cloud of smoke – less so once Father was gone, though Mother made up some of the difference by becoming a chain-smoker – so it didn't matter to me, even in this shoebox of a flat.

'He became emotionally entangled with his landlady and the landlady's daughter. He shot them, killing the mother and wounding the daughter.'

'And he was a *poet?*'

'Yes, a very fine one. The best we've had in modern times. But being a Calvinist nation, we can't bring ourselves to acknowledge this.'

'You think it's all right to murder somebody, as long as the murderer is a great poet?'

'Not at all. Achterberg was subject to certain… episodes. That's why they put him in a mental hospital rather than a prison.'

'And you and Michiel were followers of his.'

'In the sense that our work followed on from his, yes. They called us the Experimentalists. And I suppose, too, there was a kind of glamour about Achterberg. Not that we approved of murder. But, you know, he was *serious*. He wasn't playing word games.'

'I knew a man once who was capable of murder. He cracked my head on a bollard.'

'How awful.'

'I found him glamorous at first. But he was rotten company.'

'I think, in the end, that is what dismayed Michiel about Achterberg. You see he got to know him in Leusden. By then Achterberg was safely married and leading a quiet bourgeois existence. He wasn't the wild man we had excitedly imagined. Youth is monstrously unfair, of course. Pardon me.'

Michiel was snoring away in the next room. It was getting late, and I wasn't sure what I was expected to do. Go back to my flat, perhaps. Give up the sofa for Paul to sleep on. He didn't seem intent on making a move.

'It's important that you know all this.'

'It is?'

'Yes. Can I let you in on a secret?'

'That means, can you betray a confidence.'

'You're a clever bird. I think it is diffidence on Michiel's part that he has said nothing to you about it. He doesn't want to place you in an awkward position where you feel you can't say no. Not yet.'

'Go on.'

'He has made the two of us his literary executors. Given my

age, he is, in effect, entrusting his literary work and reputation – to you.'

My first thought was Aunt Ceciel. Her comment about Michiel possibly having something for me to do.

'Does this involve money?'

It was the wrong thing to say, and I didn't mean it the way it sounded. Really, I didn't. Paul answered without looking at me.

'I dare say there will be a little. Michiel has offered me my choice of his books. But we are talking about *after* his death.'

'I don't want to think about that. And I don't want to wait till then to help him. I need to find a new job, that's all, and I don't know if this is that. What did you call it again?'

'We will be his executors. Normally this would mean collecting the odd royalty or two, agreeing to have a poem appear in an anthology or whatever. But Michiel has willingly let his work slip into obscurity. There is a hunger among the young for seriousness, and he is ripe for rediscovery. It will be up to us to arrange that, if it can be arranged.'

'He might live for another twenty years.'

'I fear not. And if he won't let the doctors near him, then…'

'But he went to the hospital with you.'

'He had no choice. I found him unconscious, the door open.'

'I knew it.'

This puzzled him, but I was in no mood to explain. I don't know what mood I was in. Nobody had asked me to be a literary executor before.

'You will have to tell me all about his work. Can you do that?'

'Of course. And you must read it too. There are only the poems, and not so many of them. This was meant to be a fleeting visit, but I can't leave Michiel now, so I'm changing my plans. I have booked a room in the American Hotel for the time being.'

'Swanky.'

'Believe me, poetry isn't paying for it. A taxi will take me there shortly.'

'All right. I'll stay the night here.'

'Would you?'

'I've done that before. Michiel won't mind.'

'Good, and if he's well enough tomorrow, then perhaps we could meet in the hotel cafe and discuss things further. It would pain him to be in earshot.'

After the taxi had taken Paul away, I checked on Michiel and put another blanket over him. Then I opened the wardrobe and took out one of the books. I didn't even think about the hanging dress.

The first thing I read was the blurb again, this time imagining Paul saying it. 'A lifetime's dedication to poetry.' And now he was worried that that lifetime, of his old friend, was about to end.

I read the first poem, a short one about falling fruit, and felt nothing. Only the start of a headache. I had concentrated like this in my early schooldays, and I was a long time out of school.

I didn't waste any more time, and went straight to *M*.

There was an asterisk next to the M, and another at the foot of the page, beside the words: 'Translated from the Dutch by Marijka Clemmens, the original being the property of its inspirer.'

I flicked through without reading. Two poems per page, six pages in all. I could manage that.

It began with 'The hurt child', but I must have been rusty, because only in the second poem did I notice the 'son' that was in both of them. So, unless it was all a lie, Michiel had, or had had, a son – a son he'd never mentioned, to me. This made me sit up straight. But just as I was starting to get used to the new family arrangement, the son disappeared. I liked these two poems. I liked the dandelion seed on the breeze, and the vase of hyacinths she brings him – *she*, Madeleine. But I liked them in a way you like a stained glass picture in a church. Maybe I was being a bit too reverent, in spite of the snoring in the next room.

It's funny I should have thought of a church, because by the next poem God had put in an appearance. Stretching out his hand to Adam's. My education in the suburbs might not have been the best, but I knew my Sistine chapel. I felt pleased with myself, but, in all honesty, a bit bored already. The mention of Madeleine's white glove stirred me, but not much.

Then it started to happen. I felt the hairs on my arms and even on my thighs stir, as if a cool breeze was flowing between my clothes and my skin. And it started before the mention of

Border of Holland at the end of the fourth poem. *That* made my heart thump. The place I'd been brought to by, and then brought, all those boys in my early days was the same place he first kissed this Madeleine. Suddenly everything was real to me. And was real because, now, I could hear *him* in it. His voice, even in the English words. Speaking with that tenderness and authority I'd only ever heard from one man before. Father.

By the next poem I was weeping along with Madeleine. She wasn't only weeping, but tearing into him with her fists. Only infidelity makes a woman do this. *The bastard*, I thought, almost running next door to tear into him too. I calmed down after that, or the poems calmed down. Also I grew a bit confused, not sure if Michiel and Madeleine were or weren't married by poem seven. Surely Paul would have mentioned *that*? And then it all got heated again, and he was telling her not to cry, which meant telling me not to cry, and so I didn't. Not till it got unbearably sad, with them drifting apart, and she young and lonely, and maybe even mad by the end of it, I don't know. I never understood poetry. I always said, *If you have something to say, just say it*. But poets never seem to do that.

So why was I sitting here, confused, with wet cheeks, feeling like he'd just said it?

11

I woke to see his face above my face.

'Is that you?'

I drew up, so that the small of my back was against the cushion now. He slowly straightened.

'Where am I?'

'At home. In your living room.'

'Not in hospital?'

'No. You came back with Paul. Remember?'

'Where is he?'

'At the American Hotel.'

'He would be.'

He seemed to feel his way towards the armchair, though the room wasn't dark, or not wholly dark. I got up quickly and took my clothes into the toilet. When I came back dressed, he was asleep again. In the armchair, with his head tilted to the left. Not snoring now.

Even with no one looking, I felt a bit overdressed sitting there. Which means I was wearing a skirt. Well, I'd dressed for Aunt Ceciel. I'm sure I'd looked a sight in my skirt and blue parka, but she hadn't turned up her nose. Now, thinking about it, I'd clocked Paul's eyes straying below my waist. Yesterday was too fraught for me to care. Besides, what could these old men do? Dream, I suppose.

I clattered about the kitchen preparing breakfast, thinking it would be no bad thing if the noise woke him. He did wake, after I sat back down. Sometimes silence can be more rousing.

'So you spent the night here.'

'Yes, is that all right?'

'Of course. I will get you a sofa bed for again.'

'I'm not moving *in*.'

'But, my dear, you must.'

'I must? What about Bibi?'

'Bibi too. There is not much room, but you can walk him.'

'Can I think about it?'

'Naturally … What is that doing here?'

He had spotted his book under the head-end – *my* head-end – of the sofa.

'Paul left it for me. I was reading it before I went to sleep.'

'You needn't do that.'

'I do need to, if I'm to be your executor.'

'That little shit,' he said, bringing a fist down on the arm of the armchair.

'He's a decent man you are lucky to have as a friend. If you want *us* to be friends, then be honest and open with me, like you were just now.'

'You see? You are always right. That is why I know I made

the right choice.'

'I don't have to be always right, Paul will make the decisions. But I will do the leg work.'

'Leg work?'

'We are going to make you famous again.'

'What did I ever do to you?'

I laughed at that, but his expression was deadpan. So if fame held no appeal to him, what did?

'I read the *M* poems at the end of your book. Who is Madeleine?'

He turned his head towards me so eerily, and his face looked so stony, that I felt as if a statue had moved to take me in. The stone became ashes that a breeze from the window must have blown away. Because now I was looking at a man without a face.

'You are not to mention her.'

Now, nobody tells me what to do – ever – but I wasn't going to argue with him then. Another time, perhaps. Some time when his face couldn't slip off like that. When he was in better health, and humour. And I could talk in the right way. Not in the way of an interrogation.

'I was very moved by the poems. I wanted you to know.'

'Thank you.'

'Can I ask about Paul?'

'Why not? What about him?'

'How did you two meet?'

'I forget now.'

'He said you were in the same school of poetry.'

'Hardly.'

'He said that too. That you would never belong to any school.'

'We all have to go to school. But once you have left, there is no going back.'

'He mentioned a man called Achterberg.'

'That old devil. What did he say about him?'

'That you were disciples of his.'

'Ha!'

'And he was a murderer.'

'Did he explain about that?'

'Only that he got emotionally entangled with two women – his landlady and her daughter.'

'Vandervoort was always a sentimental fool.'

'How so?'

'People love soap opera. No, there was no *ménage a trois*. By coincidence, the landlady's daughter had the same name as a woman Gerrit *had* loved, Bep. You want to know the truth? I don't know why they don't print this. The girl walked in on Gerrit when he was masturbating. She screamed and the mother came running. Gerrit panicked, went straight for his pistol. He kept one in those days… Maybe he still did when I knew him. Whenever we quarrelled, he would look about him irritably.'

'I'm glad he didn't shoot you. Think of the stories they would have made up!'

He laughed, bending over like a man who's been winded.

When he'd recovered, he said: 'About this business of being my executor, don't worry. I have prepared everything exactly. The papers I wanted destroyed I destroyed. What's left is in order. By that, I mean, it is acceptable to me if it is published, and also that the work is literally in chronological order. Well, almost. Truth never quite keeps step with Time.'

'Where is all this?'

I must have glanced around the room, because he said: 'Not here.'

'What is it that you want me to do?'

'You will get a letter from my lawyer when I am dead. He has my instructions for you. Follow these. And if anything arises beyond the scope of my instructions, follow your instinct.'

'I'll ask Paul.'

'You won't have the chance to. The poor man is already half-eaten by cancer.'

'It can't be! His skin has such a glow!'

'It sometimes happens that way.'

I didn't ask him how he knew. Or if I did, I can't remember now. But I don't think I did. I was in a daze.

'I wish you had stayed in the hospital and let them do their tests.'

'There is nothing wrong with me.'

'Paul found you on the floor.'

'I'd had one too many, that's all.'

'But you were *unconscious*.'

'I was *asleep*.'

Now it was my turn to laugh. I felt better suddenly. Then I remembered about Paul, and felt bad again.

'I really *must* go and check on Bibi. I'll drop into Albert Heijn on the way back and get us a few things.'

'*Us?*'

'You did invite me to stay, didn't you?'

I was drenched by the time I got to the cafe in the American Hotel. Amsterdam's living room, they call it, though it's unlike any living room I've ever been in. Mother's nick-nacks weren't exactly art nouveau, and even Aunt Ceciel doesn't have stained glass in her windows. My rain-stained parka certainly drew a few glances. In fairness, the rain wasn't responsible for *all* of its stains.

The news about Paul made me think I'd find him spread out, exhausted, in one of the comfortable chairs. But no, he was standing unsupported at the reading table, licking a finger and flicking through a broadsheet.

'Hello,' I said.

'Good. You got here. Poor dear, you're soaked.'

'Building work at the Rokin. I had to wait in the rain for my tram. How are you?'

The question surprised him. *Stupid me*, I thought.

'Fine, fine. Let's have a seat.'

We sat at a table downwind from a ceiling-fan. It wasn't an accident. He repositioned his seat to feel the air more fully on his face.

He signalled to a barman-waiter in an orange waistcoat. Orange for the tourists, naturally. He ordered another espresso, and a fennel tea for me.

'It's lovely here,' I said, lying.

'I have no dependants. My money is mine to spend.'

'Quite right. How did you make it?' I couldn't help but think how differently the two old poet-friends lived. People don't choose poverty and neglect as a rule, but Michiel was the exception to most rules. And he'd had no woman to make another choice for him.

'I like your bluntness. I was a speculator, you see. Still am, off and on.'

'That doesn't sound very poetic.'

'If I had said I was a gambler, would that?'

'More so,'

'Then I am a gambler.'

I liked him, even if he wasn't my type. By that I mean my type of old man. Michiel was *that*.

'I've been thinking about your desire to help Michiel now. You are absolutely right, we can't afford to wait. So I have a proposal to make to you.'

'Go on.'

'He needs an assistant, somebody to sort out all his papers

– the various drafts of his poems, his correspondence, and so on. I'm sure they are in a frightful state. If you would agree to perform that function, then I would happily pay you a monthly stipend. Michiel needn't know anything about it. As a matter of fact, it's imperative that he doesn't. He would stop us.'

'Perhaps we should be stopped.'

'I don't believe that, and neither do you. He is a great man. If you hadn't read a single word he wrote, you would still know that.'

'And you think he will let me rummage through his papers?'

'You will have to be… artful about it,' he said, setting down his cup a little too artfully, I thought.

'All right, I'll do it.'

'We haven't agreed the terms yet.'

'Yes we have.'

I'd set my own cup down forcefully and those were the words that had come out.

'Splendid,' he said.

'But I will need some money upfront,' I said, starting really to think now.

'How much?'

'Whatever you're spending to stay here for a week.'

'Right, so.'

He drew out his wallet and began counting the bills.

'Not here,' I said, knowing how it would look.

'Oh, right,' he said, suddenly understanding. It is the sweetest thing on earth, an old man's blush.

We emptied our cups and took ourselves over to the Vondel Park. Only when he was walking did he display any frailty. At every fourth or fifth step, it seemed, his right leg would arch out, a bit like a tango dancer's. At first I thought he was kidding me. I think I even sniggered.

On a bench in the park he put the notes into my hand. Too many, as I discovered later.

'You said Michiel accused you of setting the blood hounds loose on him.'

'That's right.'

'What did he mean by that?'

'Michiel was the "Next Big Thing" once. And then he disappeared from the scene. The *M* poems stirred some of the old interest again, but he wasn't interested in any of that. There were people who were, who would have invested time and energy into restoring his reputation, but he turned all against him.'

'Not you.'

'Even me, and I'm sorry now. To be fair, two or three others remained faithful.'

'The blood hounds?'

'The remaining ones, yes. Why do you ask?'

'You must introduce me to them.'

12

What I had said to Michiel about checking on Bibi wasn't a lie. After escorting Paul back to the hotel, I took a tram – two trams – back out east. Paul had assured me that he would be with Michiel while I was gone. Not in the night, but I was less worried about the nights now. I could believe that Michiel had been asleep when Paul found him. One thing I'd learned about Michiel for sure was that he wasn't a light sleeper. And when he wasn't snoring like a beast, he was as silent as anything. Sometimes, for seconds at a time, he would stop breathing entirely.

Bibi was slow to leave Bart and come to me. I pretended not to notice – why, I don't know. Bart was slower to throw his usual accusations my way too. In fact, he didn't accuse me of anything. I couldn't bear to part with Bibi, not yet, but I could see that this was a good place for him. A house that loves dogs. Michiel's place, even if it didn't reek of old man, had a staleness to it. It was like the air never changed.

I left a letter for Kaat and Pim. My month's notice. The deposit would cover it.

I was doing everything by the book now.

The book… I took the slip of paper from my inside pocket

and dialled the number there. I made an appointment for an hour's time, which confirmed a prejudice of mine – that university people never work.

The meeting was at the Bunge House on the Spui. I'd walked past this building so many times, and only now realised that I'd been curious about it all along. Had I even noticed the young people going inside and leaving? The look was squarish in a simple way that was also ornate. Art Deco – my suburban education stretched that far.

Passing those eager young faces on the stairs – well, they weren't *all* eager, but hungry in a different way from the hungry I'd known – I could see that I'd never wanted this kind of thing for myself. There were cool-looking blue tiles just beyond my hand, so I stretched to touch them. Then I touched my cheek. This seemed strange, judging by the looks I got.

The porter's directions were good. They knew how to lay out buildings in the old days.

I saw the name and I knocked.

I was expecting another old man, but he wasn't that. He didn't have an old man's courtesy, either. He stayed in his seat behind his desk, limply offering me his hand.

'Paul Vandervoort said I should speak to you.'

'So you said.'

Not long ago I'd have turned on my heel and been out of the door already, with a killer last remark. There was too much at stake for that.

'Paul and I are Michiel de Koning's literary executors. Or will be.'

'Are you a relative of De Koning's?'

'No, a friend.'

'I see.'

What did he see? That I was an unlikely-looking friend of the great man? That I was some kind of impostor?

'Paul and I would like to end the neglect that Michiel's work has fallen into.'

He said again that he saw, adding: 'And how do you propose to do that?'

'Helped by you. And some others.'

He sighed, very audibly. I saw that there was a family photo on his desk, tilted more towards the seat I was in than towards his. A woman wearing a headscarf, with a boy and a girl.

'I've struggled for the past ten years to have De Koning included in the coursework here. I sneaked him into the "Dutch Modern Masters" course, when that was still going. Even now, I do one lecture a year on him for the course "Inventing the Self", despite the fact that none of his books is a set text. One lecture a year, and a poorly attended one at that. I've given preference to PhD applicants who included him in their proposals. Don't quote me on that. Only two made it past the selection panel. One of them was looking at the influence – the waning influence – of the Experimentalists. The other was focusing on De Koning himself. But she dropped out, never finished her thesis. So you see, that's how far I've got, in spite of all. The truth is, sadly, that the young simply don't read him. They don't see why they should.'

'Because his work is beautiful?'

'Define *beauty*. No, it isn't that simple. Even if I could prove that his work was beautiful, I would then have to justify using beauty as a criterion of judgement. In an ugly age, shouldn't art be ugly? If it is an ugly age.'

'It is.'

'Really? How do you know? Have you lived in another?'

'I've lived it in ways that you, and those people *out there*, could never live it.'

'Don't be angry. I was engaging you in debate, so you could see what I am up against. This is what academic life is like. I can't simply decide to promote Michiel de Koning *in a vacuum*. Context is all.'

'You make it sound like hell here.'

'Ah, no. That would be to place much too much importance on it.'

'Isn't there something you could be doing outside the university?'

He smiled, as if remembering something pleasant.

'I've tried that,' he said when the smile faded. 'I once ran a night class dedicated to his Madeleine poems. A kind of reading club for amateur detectives.'

'It's those poems I came to see you about,' I said, in my best business-like voice.

'Really? Why?'

'They are the ones that interest me most.'

'Yes, they do have an appeal.'

'Did your amateur detectives come up with anything?'

'All sorts. It was a lot of fun.'

'Fun?'

I felt a wave – of what? nausea? – rise in me. It wasn't fun that had brought me here. Not fun that Michiel was having in that cell-like flat.

'Oh, yes. The old devil knew what he was up to. People *love* the element of soap opera in them.'

I tried not to bristle, in so far as I could. How does one appear when one bristles? I am not a cat.

'You've met Michiel?'

'Only twice. He didn't like me.'

'He liked you enough to meet you twice.'

'True. The second time was in the company of the PhD student I mentioned. I'm sorry to report that he behaved abominably towards her.'

'That doesn't sound like Michiel.'

'It sounds exactly like him. If that isn't your experience of De Koning, you can count yourself lucky. Or blessed.'

This did make me think. He had talked about beauty as if no man had spoken like that to me before, and I did well not to reach across his too-broad desk and punch him. But this was interesting. How many sides did Michiel have?

'Did she quiz him about Madeleine?'

'He didn't give her the chance.'

'And the first time you met him?'

'That was in the Hague, at the Balkans tribunal. He was there to see the indictment of Dragan Nikolić. Nikolić was the commander of a Bosnian Serb concentration camp. It was the last place I expected to see him.'

'Why?'

'There isn't a single political line in De Koning's work. Unless you read *between* the lines. I encourage my students to do so, but they don't buy it. He just isn't political enough for them.'

'No, he's never discussed politics with me.'

It was becoming too much to take in at once, the new information about Michiel's character – not that I trusted this fool's judgement – and the picture of Michiel in a surprising setting, that arid and echoing chamber that I knew only from TV. Or had he meant the grounds of the Peace Palace? I hadn't seen those either. But I have to picture everything – it's the way I'm made, it seems. If I looked through old footage, might I glimpse Michiel standing there, a watcher in the shade?

'He discussed politics with me that day. He's quite a lefty, you know. A real firebrand. Yet none of that gets into his work. It's frustrating.'

'For you, maybe. Not everybody is political.'

'No, but studious young people are, and poetry is retreating more and more into the academy. It's a regrettable development, but that's the reality. If you want your Michiel to be read, then you will have to make a case for him to be analysed. He must be capable of bearing the weight of critical scrutiny.'

Despite his smug intention, I felt buoyed by that reference to 'your Michiel'.

'Don't you think he could bear it?'

'I'm certain that his work could. But he is a victim of… bad timing.'

'How do you mean?'

'The Achterberg people had their day. And, in the end, you know, none of them was as good as the Master himself. Not even De Koning.'

He tapped a pen briskly on his notebook as if to say, 'Case closed.'

'He says he wasn't Achterberg's disciple,' I said, opening up the case again.

'But briefly he was. And that's enough for people. They need a single clear idea to latch onto. Such as that Van Gogh cut off his own ear. Which may not even be true, apparently.'

'*M* thrilled me. It might thrill others.'

'It was a minor sensation when it first appeared. And we are talking as recently as the early 80s. Though the critical consensus is that those sonnets were written earlier.'

'Really? When?'

He relaxed a little in his seat, if he could have relaxed further.

He seemed reconciled now to not being able to usher me out of the room quickly, one hand on the small of my back.

'De Koning visited England in the mid-60s. After that, he published nothing but translations, from the English. Shakespeare, Blake, Emily Dickinson. And some odder choices, such as Laura Riding. It seemed that he fell in love with English poetry and abandoned Dutch. We know – those of us who've taken the trouble to find out – that he's led a quiet life since he came back here. Whatever those poems are about, happened in England. And they read as though written close to the events they describe. My guess is, he planned to live on in England and make a career for himself there, like the Polish writer Joseph Conrad. And that's why the poems are in English.'

'But they were written in Dutch.'

'That sly fiction? No, there were no Dutch originals, I'd happily stake my reputation on that.'

'Why would he lie?'

'It's a fiction, and as one critic remarked, fiction is only significant lying. He probably meant to write in Dutch again when he came back here, but poetry abandoned him. So he was left with these dozen poems on his hands, poems that the English-speaking world took no interest in. I happen to know that he approached *Chicago* with them.'

'Chicago?'

'*Poetry Chicago*, a famous journal. And so he invented the story that these were translations, and the originals were – how does he put it? – "the property of their inspirer". Which is a joke, right? A dig at the poet Rilke who called his famous Duino Elegies the "property" of the princess who'd let him stay at her castle.'

'So, who is the translator he mentions? Marijka somebody?'

'Marijka Clemmens. Now that *is* interesting. Clemmens was a very distinguished translator – from the Russian, mainly. Why she should have got herself involved in De Koning's little subterfuge, and allowed her own reputation to suffer as a result, is anybody's guess. To be fair to her, she didn't blacken De Koning's name. She has never actually come out and said there were no Dutch originals.'

'What if there were?'

'Impossible. There was a volume of the literary journal *Frame*, produced by Utrecht University, which featured attempts by prominent poets to re-translate the poems back into Dutch. It couldn't be done. Nobody could better the English versions. Clemmens was good, but she wasn't *that* good.'

'Is she dead?'

'No, why?'

'You speak about her in the past.'

'Her literary career is behind her now. She's turned her hand to horticulture. Something like that. She tends her garden. A very shy woman. I approached her about appearing at a translation seminar I was organising, but she wouldn't do it. Even when I promised not to bring up the *M* controversy.'

'Do you have her address?'

'It would be in my old roller deck. Hang on a minute. I don't suppose she's moved.'

But *he* moved – not nimbly. Like a person who isn't at ease inside a body. Or no, worse than that – like a street organ monkey, the one on Kalver Street. What a contrast to his smooth talk! He seemed incapable of talking and moving at the same time. Or it wasn't until he was back in his seat that he said: 'Shall we continue over lunch? At the Luden? My treat.'

I would have said no if I hadn't seen him move so jerkily. Somehow this drew the sting out of his sharp words. I almost felt sorry for him, as I did for people who wouldn't last ten minutes on the streets. Besides, I really was hungry.

We sat informally in the corner bar, that little antechamber to the restaurant for those willing to move next door and pay for a proper meal, but that was all right with me. I like the Luden, and the street it's on, the Rokin, which snakes all the way up to Dam Square. (If I had another pet, it would be a snake.) My Caesar salad and glass of red defeated his bowl of soup. Even my chair raised me above him.

It was easier listening to him while I could see breadcrumbs lodged in his teeth. His conversation was one literary judgement after another. The novelty of it kept my attention at first, but I was impatient now. Impatient to speak about Madeleine.

'You really believe she existed?'

'I *know* she did,' I said.

Now, this was hardly true, but it wiped the soupy smile off his lips.

'He told you that? Well, as the English prostitute Mandy Rice-Davies said, "He would, wouldn't he?"'

'Why would he invent her? Just to write some heartbreaking poems?'

'I don't say she is a complete invention. No, I've long argued that she is a composite figure. At least two, probably three women in one. Not to mention her role as a signifier for the city of Amsterdam.'

'Tell me about the women,' I said.

'I am completely in the dark as to who they might be, if that's what you mean. But look at the evidence of the poems. In one, he says of her, "I forgot how young you were." And this just after saying that her hair had never greyed. Well, why would it? Unless, of course, he is speaking of two women. A mother and a daughter, perhaps.'

'Like the women Achterberg shot.'

'Exactly! And that's another theory of mine. That these poems are a dig at Achterberg, a pastiche, if not a parody.'

'Then why do they make me cry, when nothing else does? I think you're wrong – Madeleine is real. I'm going to find her.'

'That's sweet, but hopeless, I'm afraid.'

'I'm not afraid. Or sweet, or hopeless. Thanks for lunch.'

He put his hand over my hand, which was pressed against the table as I got up to go.

'All right, I have some information that might help you find her.'

What was this? A trick? He seemed to enjoy resting his hand on mine. It *might* be a trick.

'I'm listening.'

'Understand that there is one important proviso to what I'm about to tell you, which is that I don't believe a word of it.'

'All right.'

'My amateur detectives came up with some interesting theories, not all of them without merit, if you suppose that Madeleine really was real, which I don't.'

'I get that. Go on.'

'One way in is to consider what might have been the nature of the scandal referred to in the eighth sonnet. That's the one beginning "Madeleine, the word is out." There were less liberal places to be than the Netherlands in the 1960s. Yet something made them flee – to England, presumably. Or to Scotland, but I'll come back to that. The second sonnet speaks of "your Antillean isles". One of my students suggested that Madeleine was a "pale Negro" from the former colonies. We know from the third sonnet that her hands were pale. Might the racial mix have been displeasing to a conservative town – to the good folk of Leusden, perhaps? It doesn't seem likely, to be honest. Still, it's worth considering. But bear in mind that those first sonnets speak of a son, and we know he didn't have children, unless of course he had a secret child. But if the son was so secret, why speak of him in a poem? It doesn't add up.'

'Is that it?'

'No, that was just one theory. And put by a rather charming girl from Aruba, so you could say that there was some projection involved there. A second theory supposes that the son also existed, that De Koning fathered the boy in Glasgow, hence the reference to the 'dear green place', which is what the word Glasgow means in Scottish Gaelic. I suppose you could check the birth records of Glasgow hospitals for 1966 or thereabouts, if you have nothing worse to do.'

'I just might.'

'I don't suppose there were too many new mothers in Glasgow called Madeleine then. If, of course, Madeleine was her name. And if it was, why didn't he call the sequence *Madeleine* rather than simply *M*? You may have to look up all the women whose name began with 'M' – possibly a trisyllabic name, with the stress on the first syllable. A name such as Margaret. Maggie, for short. That won't be so rare a name in the files there.'

'Anything else?'

'One theory we can definitely discount is that she was the daughter of Bep van Es, the girl Achterberg wounded when he killed her mother. I looked into that one myself. A relationship with Van Es's daughter might well have caused a small scandal due to the perversity of it, but there was nothing in that at all.'

'I see.'

'Which leaves only one, untested theory, as I recall. But the

woman who proposed it was really so ill – mentally ill, I mean
– that I gave it no credence at the time.'

'This sounds promising.'

'You think so? Why?'

'Because you've changed your mind about it.'

'It's true that I haven't been able to get it *out* of my mind.
But how you would ever go about proving or disproving it …'

'What did she propose?'

'She was adamant that everything in the poems is inverted,
even the letter "M", which should really be a "W". So where he
says "son", he means "daughter". De Koning and the Madeleine
of the poems had a daughter together. Perhaps they gave the
child her mother's name.'

'She was Madeleine too?'

'No, some name beginning with "W", if you follow the
theory. And so it's the *daughter* he is addressing in the tenth
sonnet. That's the one when he talks about her being "so young".
But the daughter died, and the mother went insane. Clearly,
Madeleine – the mother Madeleine – is crazy by the final
sonnet. Perhaps she took her own life. A double tragedy that
stunned De Koning into silence.'

'You believe this version, don't you?'

'No! Absolutely not!'

'Then why are the hairs on the back of your hand standing
to attention?'

13

The garden of Marijka Clemmens was concreted over. No evidence of any hand being turned to horticulture here. So much for academic rigour!

What kind of unreliable world had I strayed into? It was a world made out of words.

Marijka herself was solid flesh and blood. Birdlike, yes, but sharply real, and quick in her movements. A bird with a broken beak. We sat outside at a garden table, under an unneeded shade.

I'd only had to mention Michiel's name in my phone call for her to invite me over.

I was here to quiz her, but an hour passed in which only I spoke. Or so it seemed. Telling the story of my encounter with Michiel and what had transpired since. She smiled or nodded approval at odd moments – smiles and nods of recognition. Even when I spoke of his injections.

'We are from a different era,' she said at last. 'In our heyday we thought nothing of taking valium to overcome our initial block, and then amphetamines to speed up the writing process.'

'You were a writer too?'

'A translator, but I approached the task in a writerly fashion.'

'They say your translations of Michiel's *M* are unbeatable.'

I'd taken a risk, and I knew it. She piped down just as she'd piped up. It was startling to watch. To see her tuck in her head, exactly as a bird does. Should I look away to stop my eyes being pecked?

'I'm sorry,' I said. 'Did I say something wrong?'

'No, dear. It is just that it is difficult for me.'

'But I love those poems,' I said. 'I don't care if they were written first in Dutch, or only in English. Really I don't.'

'I believe you. But, you see, *I* care. Very deeply.'

She went inside to make more tea. She took longer this time, though there was less to prepare. I imagined she was collecting her thoughts, or gathering up her strength. Who else in these parts would ask her about Michiel de Koning? A whole year might pass with no mention of him. And no day with no thought of him.

'What is the truth?'

'You dare to ask me that?'

'Is it really so daring a question?'

'Do you think I would lie about such a grave matter.'

'Are poems grave?'

'Michiel's are. You ought to know *that*.'

Clearly angry with me, she still managed to pour the tea into my cup gracefully and with a steady hand. She was old-school, like Aunt Ceciel, only not quite. *Bohemian* old-school.

'Can we talk about the poems and what they mean?' I asked.

'The Madeleine poems?'

'It's interesting you should call them that. I was talking to Evert Rosenkrans. He wondered why Michiel used the title *M* rather than *Madeleine.*'

'And did he have any theories about that? Evert loves his theories.'

'Yes, he did,' I laughed. 'Or one of his students did. She said it was really a "W".'

'Well, that gets us nowhere.'

'And that when he mentions a son he really means his daughter.'

'Goodness. That's not how I read the poems. Not at all.'

'He didn't have a son, though, did he?'

'Nor did the homosexual poet Garcia Lorca, who wrote, "Once I had a son named John." I used to think that those first poems in the sequence were merely conventional, like the first of William Shakespeare's sonnets, which exhort his male lover to marry. Michiel knew his Shakespeare very well. Shakespeare didn't really mean it, and neither did Michiel. But now I have a different take on those first two Madeleine poems. They are very tender, especially the second. I think he was speaking both to his younger self and to an imagined future son.'

'So the poems *were* written much earlier than they appeared?'

'Not only written much earlier, translated too. He came to me with the poems on the 20th of July, 1969. How can I be so sure? It was the day of the moon landing. I watched it on television that same night, after he'd left. Can you imagine? He had no interest in seeing it.'

Yes, I could imagine. I had to imagine everything.

'Did he explain the poems to you?'

She looked me up and down.

'He said nothing. He came to my house (not this one), gave me the poems and one afternoon in which to translate them. He lay the whole time smoking on the sofa while I sat at the dining table with nothing but a pen and notepaper. Not even a dictionary was permitted. He did let me have a brandy, I remember that. I needed it.'

'And you produced these amazing versions which no other poet can translate back into Dutch – in those conditions?'

'Well, I'll tell you something about that. The versions I produced are not the versions that appeared. Not exactly. Not even approximately, in one or two instances. Michiel must have worked on them afterwards. He would have needed to.'

'Is that so shocking?'

'Ha! You are a good girl.'

For the first time, I looked around me. The garden was concreted over, yes, but it was edged by bushes and a few elm trees. They looked... maybe not diseased, but sickly.

'No, it isn't shocking,' she said. 'But he gave me all the credit, you see, and I didn't deserve it all. Nor all the blame. I asked him to let me set the record straight, but he said, "Say nothing".'

'And you obeyed. Till now.'

'Until now. But you are his literary executor, so it's right you should know. Please don't reveal this until after Michiel's death. It won't harm his reputation, only mine.'

'Can you remember what was different about the versions you produced.'

'No, I can't. But I know there are lines, and parts of lines, I could never have written. I would never have used the word "tilth", for instance. That's a very old-fashioned English word, maybe even obsolete now. And those lovely lines:

A quiet summerhouse, some dear green place
Where the dragonfly whirrs uneven wings

That kind of thing is quite beyond me, or I would have been a poet myself.'

'Evert says the "dear green place" could be Glasgow, in Scotland.'

'Evert thinks all writing is a code he must crack.'

'He also says Madeleine isn't a real person.'

'What do you say?'

'That only a man could think that.'

'Now, now. It was, after all, a man who wrote the poems. Madeleine was very real.'

'You knew her?' The hairs on my arms were paying attention now.

'Not as such. But I was close to Michiel, as close as any

woman who wasn't actually intimate with him. I saw him before he left for England – a troubled man, but wholly alive – and when he returned. He came back absolutely desolate. I've never seen anyone so desolate outside of a madhouse.'

'Did Madeleine go mad?'

'I see no other way of reading the final poem. But Evert may be right in that Madeleine is unlikely to have been her real name. Michiel was fascinated by Gnosticism, he even wore a Gnostic ring, and would have known well the Gospel According to Mary Magdalene. Madeleine is a form of Magdalene, you know. According to Levi in that Gospel, the Lord loved her best of all.'

'Wouldn't that mean Michiel seeing himself as Christ?'

'Isn't the power of Christianity that we all do? Each of us is crucified, in one way or another.'

'I'm not a Christian,' I said.

'You are young.'

This riled me. What riled me more was that I hadn't registered, till now, the delicate cross on the bare wall that was visible through the kitchen window. I needed to be sharp to get to the truth. Maybe Evert wasn't wrong. Maybe it *was* all a code.

'Have you told anybody else what you've told me?'

'No. Never.'

'Then why me?'

'Because you are his executor. I explained that.'

'Paul Vandervoort is too. May I tell him?'

'Dear, sweet Paul. I think you shouldn't. He's a loyal friend to Michiel.'

'And I'm not?'

'I don't mean to offend. It is just that Paul and Michiel go back a long way. Though I don't think Paul ever really understood his old friend. His criticism is often wide of the mark. But no, it's best he doesn't hear, not yet. You know how chivalrous and silly these men can be. Has no one in the family been appointed also?'

'Michiel has a family?'

'Well there's his brother Jaap, for one. Not that he is very *simpatico*.'

'I'd like to meet him.'

'He has a house in Eindhoven. I visited him once to ask after Michiel. That was ten, perhaps eleven, years ago.'

'Why didn't you come to Amsterdam and see Michiel for yourself?'

'I never knew his address. You see, he always contacted *me*. And then he didn't.'

'I'm sorry.'

She smiled at that, as at a thought.

'There's another reason why I confided in you,' she said. 'And that's because you are not *one of them*.'

'One of who?'

'Those boys like Evert with their puffed-out chests and their silly ideas.'

'I've really enjoyed today. Thanks.'

I was already standing up. I didn't mean to be rude, but my mind was racing towards Eindhoven.

'Please give Michiel my best wishes,' she said, and set my cup back on the tray.

'I'll give him your love,' I said, turning to go.

14

I was on a train hurtling through dark fields when it occurred to me that Michiel's brother might not be in the phone book. The first thing I did after checking into the hotel was ask to see one. Checking into the Crown without a bag or a credit card wasn't easy, but I had enough cash to make the concierge overlook my stained parka, and whatever else about me these guys overlook. Lo and behold, Jaap de Koning wasn't just there but was the only name in bold on the page. So he had paid extra to publicise himself. Not a bit like his brother, then.

Except, of course, that this might not be him. Today had emboldened me, and so I called immediately, from the phone in the lobby. It was him all right. After a silence he confirmed it, adding only: 'What do you want?' I wanted to meet him. He didn't want to meet me, that was obvious, even as he said to come round in the morning. *After* eleven.

I lay on top of the thin duvet and flicked through the TV channels. TV has never interested me – I struggle to follow the thread of any programme, except cartoons. Should Michiel de Koning's legacy really be in my hands? But then, wasn't Madeleine's legacy in *his* hands? Might mine be in his hands too

– or in some others'? I picked up the complimentary notepad.

In my spidery handwriting, which even I struggle to read, I wrote:

Theories about M:
- Had Michiel's son in Glasgow (dear green place) in mid-60s
- Everything the wrong way round, even M, so had a daughter not a son.
- Son (or daughter) not true
- Is black, Dutch Antilles, and pale, so 'word is out' = shocked locals (would Michiel care?)
- Is some other name, Margaret, Magdalene
- Is the daughter of Bep van Es, the girl A. shot (check this out, E. not to be trusted)
- Is two women, mother and daughter
- Went mad (don't assume this)

If only I had Michiel's book with me. Already undressed – I had to keep my clothes from smelling awful – I lay under the thin duvet, and put off the lights, one switch after another. With my eyes shut tight, I could see them: the words, black on white on black, with only the white shifting, milkily. Not every word of every poem, but enough, and some from each, though the eleventh was blank except for the words 'the Black Rider'. Maybe my hands were the wrong ones for the job, but not my eyes.

Black. And white. One line grew large in the dark. 'Your hand, so pale within the white, so pale.' What did it remind me of?

Africa. And a toy snake. And, gently patting me and ushering me out, the white-gloved hand of Father's secretary.

Could Madeleine have been that – a secretary? Had Michiel fallen, as so many men have done, for his own secretary?

I thought of – no I didn't, I *saw* – the red ketchup on the wall. Saw again Father's unguilty, determined look. And heard Mother's stifled sobbing. Not all that stifled. Her jealousy of his white-gloved secretary.

It didn't keep me awake.

That night I dreamt of her. I've dreamt of her since, but that night was the first time. The best dream I ever had. I don't know who or what she was. Not some secretary. A goddess maybe. Maybe the Mother of God, who knows?

At breakfast, remembering my dream, I even cried a little. My few tears splashed on a blue napkin that had a single row of hemstitching. I was stirring a pot of Dutch Lady Yoghurt.

I'd been to Eindhoven before. An overdesigned bombsite cleanup. Somebody's idea of the future once. Here I was, with an hour to kill, looking at buildings again. I went into a museum that was nothing like my old colonial one opposite the burnt-out church. In it I flicked through an end-exam catalogue of the Willem de Kooning academy.

I wasn't feeling quite myself today. Yesterday was taking its toll.

I took a taxi to the brother's house. It was a flat, in fact, though most of the building was his. So he told me before I'd even sat down.

There was no doubting the family resemblance, though this brother was stockier, less willowy. And yet he was the elder. A man who had taken care of himself, clearly. Whose bookshelves were well dusted, if not by him.

By whom, then? I could see no signs of a wife and no photos of children.

'Is your wife here?' I asked, and read surprise in his face.

'You are blunt,' he said. 'My wife is with my son on the floor below. They won't disturb us.'

'Good,' I said, though I didn't mean 'good'. Or I meant, it was good that he had a wife and a son. There is, as Aunt Ceciel never tires of saying, someone for everyone.

'What do you want to know?'

'I've been appointed Michiel's literary executor.'

'Have you, indeed?'

'Yes. Together with Paul Vandervoort.'

'Insufferable little man,' he said.

'You are blunt yourself.'

'Go on.'

'We are hoping to reignite interest in Michiel. I am especially interested in his poems called *M*.'

'Oh, another one.'

'Pardon?'

'I had a woman here before asking about them. About *her*.'

'Madeleine.'

'As if I keep track of my brother's sex life!'

'I think there was more to it than just sex,' I said.

'You were there, were you?'

'Hardly.'

'And are you his latest – what is it they call your kind? – *Muse*?'

'I'm a friend of Michiel's, and his literary executor.'

'He never mentioned you.'

'You've spoken to him recently?'

'A few days ago. He was asking to be forgiven. I'm not sure what for. I don't think *he* was.'

'Didn't you go to see him?'

'Didn't think to, no. I expect he had hit the bottle.'

'He isn't just some drunk,' I said, stirred to defend him.

'For a man who hasn't done an honest day's work in his life, Michiel attracts an impressively loyal band of followers.'

'And what's your line of work, if I may ask?' I was trying to cool my cheeks now.

'Oh, business. All that is in the past.'

'Your father was a diplomat, wasn't he?'

'Yes, that's right,' he said, softening a little – at least, I *wanted* to think so. 'He would have liked us to follow in his footsteps.

Mother would have liked it too. But I cared for money too much, and Michiel cared… well, whatever it is he cares for.'

'Poetry?'

'Being *adored.*'

I knew well the kind of man who cares for adoration, and that this wasn't Michiel.

'You don't like your brother much, do you?'

'You don't have to like the fellow beside you in the trenches. And when the war is over, you needn't keep in touch.'

'So, for you boys, life was war?'

'Not at all. Very sedate, in fact. And prosperous too. It was Michiel's choice to live among riff-raff.'

'Why do you hurt me?'

He looked at me directly for only the second time. It felt like he really did see me this time and, despite the rheumy eyes, with as piercing a look as his brother's.

'Because I am an old man who has seen too much. Do you understand?'

'No, I don't.'

A loud groan came from below. It startled me, but not Jaap.

'Ignore me,' he said, meaning 'Ignore that'.

'Do you know who Madeleine was?'

'Yes.'

'You do! Who?'

'They came here on the way to the ferry. Wanting money, of course. I gave it to them.'

'What was she like? Young? Black?'

'Black? I shouldn't think so. She was young, I couldn't say how young. Not enough to be his *daughter*.'

This was directed at me, I knew, but I didn't rise to it.

'Was she good-looking?'

For the third time he looked directly at me.

'I've never seen a more captivating woman,' he said, as quietly as his booming voice allowed.

'And what happened to her?'

'Who knows? The next time I saw Michiel he had another one on his arm.'

'When was that?'

I wanted to know, but also to cover up my surprise. Michiel was no better than a dandy, if his brother was to be believed.

'Ten years later, on the Kalver Street. They ducked into a leather goods shop. I should have followed them inside and said *Boo!*'

'Perhaps he wants forgiven for that.'

'Yes, perhaps that's it.'

'Has nobody asked you about this before?'

'That one lady.'

'Did she have a harelip?'

'She had very thick lipstick, I remember that.'

'And did you tell her what you told me?'

'I might have. Can't remember now. Is the interrogation over?'

'Not quite. Are you certain that the woman Michiel brought here was Madeleine?'

'So she said.'

'*She* said?'

'Michiel hadn't the decency to introduce us. He was only interested in the money, you see.'

'How much did you give him?'

'Not what he asked for, but enough.'

'Did he pay you back?'

'Of course not. Perhaps he wants forgiven for that too.'

Only as I stepped back into the daylight did I realize how dark it had been inside. He was still holding open the door, dazed by the kiss I had given him. A moment's kiss on the cheek. Which he had done everything he could to prevent.

At ground level I heard the groan again. I saw, in the window, looking out at me, a severely disabled man. So he must have been, judging by the contraption he sat in. Then I saw an old woman place her hands on his head.

15

The thing is, not to be broken.

And not to go mad.

On the Amsterdam train I kept thinking about his insult. I was nobody's fool, nobody's *muse*.

So, she was really real. They had fled one night, one blazing night, catching the ferry over the dark waves to England. Something happened there to make him desolate.

But they had come back. Both. *After our exile, our return.* Where was she now? *Was* she now?

The most captivating woman he'd ever seen. He didn't say beautiful.

Here were the fields in daylight. The neat geometry of it all. Of a land that should be submerged by the sea. The dark waves of the sea.

I am lost. And alone.

I should have gone back to him. Straight away. Not bothered to shower and change in my flat. The flat I was leaving. My poor dear Bibi wasn't even there, was being walked.

My conscience is clear. I keep telling myself this.

I thought of the boy I'd seen dangling from a bar in the little play area. That first time I had visited. He wasn't there, of course he wasn't. As I was adjusting to the thought of this, a little girl appeared. On the path the witch had swept.

The little minx blocked my way.

'Excuse me,' I said.

'What do you want?'

I almost laughed to hear her say it. Jaap's remark on the phone, and spoken just as solemnly. Just as if she was impersonating him.

'I want to see my friend, Michiel,' I said, as if she had a right to know.

'Why are you looking for him here?'

'Because he lives here.'

'No. They took them.'

Panic isn't blind. This panic wasn't. With it came the words *I knew it, I knew it*, like tolling bells.

'Who took him?'

'Ambulance men.'

'When?'

'After the siren stopped.'

'Leave the child alone,' I heard a voice say, and spun round to see a woman standing next to me. It was then I saw that I was holding the girl.

'The two old men fell sick and were taken to hospital,' the woman said, ushering the girl towards her.

'At the same time?'

'An accident never comes alone, I suppose.'

'I need to see,' I said. But all I saw when I got beyond the open red door was the closed grey one. I hammered on it all the same. When I got back to the street the woman and the girl were gone.

I waited, walking up and down and across and back, at the tram stop, till I remembered I had plenty of cash for a taxi. I got into a minicab, which is something I don't do. I know too many horror stories.

I forgot Paul's surname. In my head on the way to the hospital I was rehearsing what to say, and I forgot his name. But it was Michiel I was interested in. Nobody is equal when it comes down to it.

'Michiel de Koning,' I said to the registrar. 'And Paul Vandervoort,' I added, inspired. 'Two old men who fell ill at the same time. Not old, in their seventies.'

It wasn't visiting time, I was told, and both were gravely ill. This was repeated to me outside the ward.

'Mr De Koning,' the doctor said. 'Has he had an injury to his head recently?'

'I don't know. Did he fall yesterday?'

'There is no indication that he sustained any injury yesterday. But there has been serious internal bleeding in the skull in the recent past. Are you his daughter?'

'Yes,' I said, not wanting to be excluded suddenly.

'Then you may soon have to prepare for the worst. He is rather frail for surgery, but without it there is a risk of severe haemorrhage.'

'Can't you operate anyway?'

'That would require his consent for as long as he is capable of giving or withholding it. He says he wants to go home to die. When he is no longer capable of deciding, then we will require the written consent of his next of kin. Is that you?'

'Yes,' I said, feeling a net closing in on me. 'But I need to speak to his brother in Eindhoven. I can phone him now.'

'Do. The sooner, the better.'

'Can I not see Michiel? I might be able to persuade him.'

'All right, but contact the brother first, if you need to.'

'I'll do that now.'

There was a bank of phones near the entrance hall, which I passed on my way out. I thought I needed fresh air in my lungs before deciding whether to call. But I had already decided. Michiel's brother had been useful to him once, but not any more. Endings *ought* to be sudden.

The doctor was gone but he had instructed the ward nurse to let me pass.

Michiel's darling head, propped on many pillows, was set at too high an angle from his body. I worried that his neck would snap like a flower stem.

'I am dying,' he said.

'I know.'

'Will you let me?'

'Yes.'

'Good. Then we can go.'

Nothing in a hospital is easy, and this wasn't. Michiel was within his rights to discharge himself, we told the ward nurse.

'Not if your life is in imminent danger. You will have to wait to be examined first.'

'He's just been examined,' I said.

'You will have to wait.'

We waited, talking the whole time, a bit oddly. It was pleasant to be led astray by him.

'Where is Paul?' he asked during a lull.

'I don't know which ward he's in.'

'*Ward?*'

It didn't occur to me that he wouldn't know of Paul's collapse, if that's what it was. He was extremely agitated.

'Find out where he is. I'll get dressed,' he said, pressing a button in the panel.

When I came back, he did have his clothes on but they looked misshapen somehow. He was in a wheelchair, swatting away the ward nurse.

'I'll bring him back,' I said, steering him through the wide doors. In my time away from Michiel, I had located Paul's ward. I told him so.

'Well?'

'In here.'

'What a couple of clowns we are,' he said to his fraily smiling friend as I parked him by the bed head.

'Michiel.'

'Don't get up,' Michiel said, with that dark humour old friends share.

'Not sure I ever will again. You managed.'

'The calm before the storm we both know's coming.'

'Mine has arrived, dear friend.'

'Yes.'

I hadn't spoken, but now I said: 'I'm taking Michiel home.'

'Home is the best place. It will be a hospice for me.'

'But only yesterday you were…'

'Dear girl. All that is in the past, as I will be.'

'I don't see why,' I said.

'One never does.'

I bowed out of the conversation at this point, without moving. It felt strange, felt good, to be on the sidelines for this.

'We had an interesting time, didn't we, Michiel?'

'We did.'

'I'm sorry it didn't work out for you… over there.'

Michiel waved his hand.

'Forgive me for not having been a better friend.'

'Likewise.'

'Here we are, trying to say the most important things. Unable to.'

'We said them in our poems.'

'You did. I never succeeded.'

'Even one good line is a kick against the pricks,' Michiel said, half in English.

'Did I write one?'

'Yes.'

'Remind me.'

I thought for an awful moment that Michiel wouldn't manage, till he said: 'Love has gnawed us to the bone.'

'That isn't too shabby, now.'

'I always wished I'd written it.'

'Well, there. Praise indeed. Do you think …'

With more life in his body, he would have doubled over from his fit of coughing.

'No more talk,' Michiel said, patting Paul's hand, as a nurse approached. I got up and moved to the windowsill.

16

'Are you ready for this?'

I carried the tray over to his bed – his own bed, at last. The pillows were propping up his back this time.

'Herring,' I said.

'Where did you get this?'

'In a jar at the back of the cupboard. I couldn't see any date on it, but anyway they last forever.'

I sat on the bed next to him, facing the wall and watching him eat. He didn't seem to mind. After a while, I helped him with the fork. It got awkward as he slipped further down the bed.

'A drink to wash it down.'

'Oh, sorry. I'll get some water.'

'Talisker,' he said, giving me a look that warned me not to defy him.

'Robert Louis Stevenson's favourite,' I said, and he smiled. With the eyes as much as the lips. A good sign, I thought.

The glass was fairly full. Again, I helped him.

'Can we not talk?' he asked.

'All right.'

I performed all the tasks required of me, and eventually he

slipped so far down that he was in a perfect position to fall sleep, which he did. I sat on, enjoying the stillness and the silence.

Whatever had happened to Michiel and Paul had happened here. Much of the wardrobe's contents was spilled out onto the floor, books included, so I didn't feel such a thief picking one up this time. I picked *all* up, tidying them away. The wardrobe rail was broken, and a corduroy suit was off its hanger and the diamond-patterned dress half out of its bag. I took both and hung them from the curtain rail in the living room. There were papers too, ones he hadn't squirrelled away somewhere with the rest. And photos.

I could never resist looking at photos. That's why I don't keep any. I don't want my past clinging to me.

He must have been more sentimental.

I got to see his mother and his father. His mother was a great beauty except that she had a squint. It only added to her beauty in my eyes, but I know the world doesn't see through those. And Jaap was just as fierce-looking when he was a toddler. There was one of him reaching up to a pram which presumably contained Michiel. It seemed just as well that his arms weren't long enough.

The oldest photos were intact, but some of the more recent – that is, decades old – looked almost bleached white. There was one that had just faint outlines of bodies above the waist, three bodies, which below the waist were clearly those of two women and a man. The women's legs were exquisite, crossed in a way that showed the women *knew*. The man could have been Michiel – if he had changed his taste in trousers and shoes over the years. When I turned the photo over, it was as if I'd been plugged into the wall. On the back, in faint blue pen, was the word 'Dormansland' and the year – 1966.

I moved the photo into the light of the window, and received a second jolt. There was mad Mina, looking in, not sweeping, from her patch of pavement. I made a face as if to scare her away, but you can't frighten a witch.

The third jolt was in my head.

I strode, almost ran, outside.

'You're her, aren't you? You are M and also W. Mina, Wilhelmina. You are Madeleine!'

She looked through me, as only children or the mad can do.

'Idiot girl,' she spat.

I ran back inside and closed the curtains as best I could, with my eyes unfocused so I wouldn't see her. My heart was pounding. I've felt my heart pounding before and been glad of it. Cleansed, almost. But not this time. Something wasn't right.

A revelation should make all seem right, but something here was wrong. Was I wrong? If Mina was Madeleine, who was the other he rejected her for? *Could* Michiel ever have rejected Madeleine?

In the bedroom, I watched him sleeping. I thought it would calm me. I started to think it *was* calming me – thought I imagined a breeze at my back.

Sometimes you think you are only imagining what is really real.

'Hello,' a child's voice said.

I shot round. It was the girl from before.

'Why were you shouting at Mina?'

'I wasn't shouting.'

'Yes you were.'

'What are you *doing* here?'

'The door was open.'

I had closed the curtains but not the door.

'What's your name?'

'Fransiska.'

'Well, Fransiska, Michiel is very, very sick, and I need to look after him now.'

'I can help you,' she said.

'That's sweet of you, but I'm fine as I am.'

'You don't look fine.'

'Don't I?'

'You look mad.'

'Won't your mummy be wondering where you are?'

'She knows I'm playing.'

'This isn't play,' I said.

'Id-i-ot girl,' she sang, and skipped out.

I closed the door after her. Had I closed it too firmly? Michiel was awake.

'What?' he said, and again, 'What?'

'It's all right,' I said, going back to my spot on the bed.

'Why won't you let me sleep!'

'It's all right, Michiel,' I said, attempting to stroke his head. He swatted me away, as he'd done the nurse, only more powerfully. That surprised me.

'Let me sleep!'

He rose up like a demon. Vomit shot out of his mouth and onto my face. Only, a second later I saw that it wasn't vomit, or not only that. A lungful of blood and a stomachful of vomit, over my hair, my face, my neck, my chest, my arms.

He sank back down, gargling the remnants in his throat.

He was dead, I knew he was dead. And then he moved. Slipped to the side. A corpse can do that.

I ran, but not outside. I ran to the bathroom and wiped off whatever the hand towel could absorb. And then I ran outside.

It wasn't even night. Not properly. Nobody should die except in the night. But it was getting late. I was right to have chased Fransiska back to her mummy.

I wanted to disappear behind the light. I so wished it was night.

You strangers are always there, judging me. Haven't any of you run out on a corpse? You are all so mild-mannered I could scream.

I didn't want the park or its iron gates. Or the museum which was shut anyway.

The church. The burnt-out church.

Who knows what strength is in any of us? I broke the boards and punched a hole in the door with my bare hands. Which were bleeding now. His blood and my blood.

I didn't care who saw, and nobody stopped me. I was inside at last. The great cavern I thought would be there wasn't. None of that. Only the altar-end.

My God the place stank.

I was down on my hands and knees in the dirt.

17

It is a ten-minute walk from the church to Transval Street. Though the road seems straight as an arrow in this flat land, you can't see one from the other. And you always think you should have arrived sooner than you do.

I expect you expect I should have been blind to it, but no, I took it all in. Every little detail that you wouldn't want to hear. You never paid that much attention. Can you pay it now? Can you?

I didn't look in on him. I took off all my clothes and balled them together. And I showered.

In the living room I put on the dress. I always knew I would.

Then I went to him. He was sitting up and he was glowing.

'You came back,' he said.

I sat on the side of the bed that was free of blood.

'Who was she? Who was Madeleine?'

'A secretary.'

'Yours?'

'No, I never had one.'

'Ah.'

'There was also another one. Her friend.'

'Two!'

'The friend was pregnant.'

'And you were the father.'

'No. But they all thought so.'

'They?'

'The department. I was with two young women and one was pregnant.'

'What happened?'

'The friend went to England and we followed.'

'Dormansland.'

'Yes. I found work nearby.'

'Who did you love?'

'Madeleine. But I was fond of the other. And the child.'

'The child is why you go to the hyacinth bed once a year.'

'Yes.'

'What was her name?'

'It was a boy. But the girl they found in the park had the same birthday. She died on it. That touched me.'

'The boy was disabled, wasn't he?'

'You knew?'

'What happened to them?'

'The woman and the boy stayed in England. For a while.'

'Madeleine?'

'Her family took care of her. They had experience of that kind of thing.'

'You've never tried to find her?'

'Everything has its season.'

'That's a lie.'

'You're free to think so.'

'I'm not free.'

He closed his eyes and opened them again. The glow was fading.

'I'm dying, Femke.'

'Shh. No more talk.'

I held his head to my breast and sang.

Sail your boat, drink your tea.
We're sailing to the Overtoom.

I don't know how long I sang for. Not long. After a while I knew I was singing only to myself.

She says she wants to put make-up on dead people for a living. She loved looking at Michiel in the coffin. I tell her that, at six, I wanted to be a hairdresser like my mother. Her mother doesn't do anything, she says. I say I am responsible for Michiel's literary legacy, and when she asks me what that is, I say, 'His books.'

The bookcase is the one thing I haven't touched yet. Even the whisky bottle is where it was – behind a book of Vondel's plays *David in Exile* and *David Restored*. I don't feel tempted to drink from it, though I could pull out the cork and sniff that to remind myself. There used to be a cork mat outside the shower, showing the shape of his dripping feet. Whisky and cork and Marlboro smoke – when I smell these I know he hasn't gone away.

I found his cane. The old fool had hidden it away. I've kept it hidden.

For superstitious reasons, and because no one is looking for me anyway, I have kept his name on the intercom buzzer, which never worked. It isn't even his name, just the initials, MdK, in blue ink faded long ago. Maybe it's a kind of headstone – there isn't another. Nothing to show. That was him all over.

I never made it to Paul Vandervoort's funeral. It was in the south, and I had a meeting with Michiel's lawyer that day. The lawyer gave me the address of the storage facility where Michiel's papers are being kept, and the pin code of the storage unit. He could arrange to keep up the monthly payments for this and bill me annually. I said I would take care of all that. I've never had this much money before, and I'm determined to make good use of it. I have the cost of the flat now, but since Jaap de Koning refused the money I offered the son, there is plenty left over.

I make sure I bring lots of provisions when I visit Fransiska's family. The little ones – there are two younger than Fransiska – even call me Auntie. The mother hardly gets out of the kitchen – somebody is always yelping for more of something. I tidy up the toys before I leave, and that pleases her.

She's happy for me to take on the girl, even to have her sleep over from time to time. The bed and the blood-stained carpet had to go, and now I have a bed that's so wide there isn't room for any wardrobe, only a set of drawers at its foot. I do fill these now. I've acquired some clothes that don't single me out when I'm walking. I never thought I'd *want* to blend in. Things do change, after all.

One thing that's different about me is that my trances have stopped. I know they've stopped because Fransiska would tell me if they hadn't. She tells me everything. If I have lipstick on my teeth, or odd socks on, or a hair-clip out of place. And when she tells me I haven't listened to her, I know it's because I've been thinking of something else. Usually something that might happen, not something that did. That's different too.

It's nice to have company on my walks with Bibi now. My morning walks, not the evening ones. In the morning I go over all my old routes and tell Fransiska about my life. Sometimes I tell her the real story, and other times I'm more careful. She has a nose for those other times. 'No, no,' she says, 'don't tell a fib.' I don't think it does much harm to know adult stuff ahead of time. I used to eavesdrop on Mother's conversations with her clients. It wasn't hard – they had to talk above the dryer. I heard a lot of stuff about what men and women got up to in the suburbs. It wasn't all daytime TV watching. In the evenings, when Fransiska is with her family, I avoid the park. I didn't at first, till I kept thinking something awful was about to happen there. Best to trust a feeling like that.

This morning I met a man who crossed over to the building I used to clean. He was well-dressed but not too formal, had a black computer bag in his hand. Must have been a teacher there. I caught his eye – I could tell. For a second it was as if I'd left my body and entered his. I wanted to see what his life was like. I know what my own's like. I really think I do now.

The slower pace suits Bibi now – to tell the truth, it suits me too. Bart was so broken-hearted to lose Bibi I said he could come round whenever he likes. He hasn't yet, but he said he would.

I keep meaning to drop in on Evert Rosenkrans. The bibliography he gave me doesn't quite match the list of Michiel's works mentioned in the storage papers. I expect this is normal. I'll chase it up, but it's harder to make appointments, with Bibi and now Fransiska to look after.

I've let go of my need to know about Madeleine. People are only mysterious from a distance, or if you get too close. I have to trust Michiel's instinct. Besides, he isn't here to restore to health any more. I see now that she couldn't have done that. He didn't manage it for her. I didn't manage it for him.

I scooped up all the loose change from the bottom of every drawer, and put it in a big bag for Fransiska. She loves the old guilder coins. To her, they represent ancient history. The Antilles guilder is her favourite. I must say, Beatrix looked well in 1992. I thought, when I saw it again, 'Mother could have done her hair.'

One day I'll have Aunt Ceciel round to tea.

The next thing I have to do is pay my respects at the hyacinth bed. How strange it will be to have Fransiska beside me on the bench. I've decided we'll bring a picnic so that she has good memories of the day and not sad ones. A child shouldn't be sad.

M*

Michiel de Koning

I

The hurt child who's mistaken for a sage
Will have the elders nodding in agreement
As they plot his death… Go, son, act your age:
Your mother's slip is not a priestly vestment.

Enamoured of the strength of the long-haired,
You've had your nose too long in that big book.
All who stopped there have, in the end, despaired:
You want to avoid their pinched, thin-lipped look.

It's not too late: the boats dance in the water,
The dandelion seed drifts on the breeze.
Squint at the sun – summers will not be hotter –
Or chase a ball with bruised and bloodied knees.

Don't fret, not in the slightest, about sin.
Ahead of you lies death, and Madeleine.

* Translated from the Dutch by Marijka Clemmens, the original being the
property of its inspirer.

2

I am not my son. My son says: I am
Not my father. And yet I make the boy
(God forgive me) assume my martyrdom
At your hands. Madeleine, no silken joy
Runs through my grief that time has separate shores
On which to strand us. Long washed up, I see
You come into your own. My blue Azores
Match your Antillean isles to a T,
Save in age. (Every schoolboy understands
The need to tease the elders as they probe
In dark.) You even now reach out your hands,
Your hands that cast no dice and rent no robe,
But bring me hyacinths from the meadow
And put them in a vase, and set them so.

3

The sun and wind and all the planet's filth
Conspire to weather our extremities.
Some people, darkened by the heat of tilth
Or else a spot of gardening on their knees,
Scrub and scrub the dirt to their heart's content.
Your hand, so pale within the white, so pale
And gestureless, reminds me what was meant
By God when he made Adam firm and hale
With outstretched arm. Reject me, Madeleine,
And be a Muse to God. I'll only lie
To get my man's deserts, and call you mine,
And never once guess that you are lonely.
It's your pale hand in a white glove's mysterious;
Touched, and the dart of longing will be His.

4

You play a game. A game of memory.

What was the weather like when we first kissed?

How many tram stops to the brewery

Where your small flat was? (Does it still exist?)

Who spoke the word 'love' first? In which month? Where?

What was our first row about? Who invented

The curtain-signal?

                Love, I stroke your hair

And leave the answers that you crave unsaid,

Not because, as you suppose, I can't play

The game as well as you – let's be grown-up

About it – but because my memory

Is so strong, really so strong, it might rip

Us both to pieces. You think not? Stormy,

Six, you, May, Hollandsche Rading, her, me.

5

You came back when the gas was at a peep
And stared into my eyes as if you knew,
And, naturally, you did know. The steps were steep,
And you were breathless, still, and then you flew
And wounded me, quite rightly – first my head
And then my chest, my gut, lastly my groin –
And wept, and said you wished that I was dead
And then wished you were … I could only join
Your hands together, placing my own on top,
Whisper again the Malay word for milk
Which soothed you once before, till you said 'Stop,'
Unknotted the red ribbon of pure silk
And gave a better gift – your loosened hair
That's never greyed, through all your great despair.

6

There is an old, old woman made of stone
Watching over you, and at your window
She'll sign to the Black Rider you're alone
With a curtain's twitch. Then a man will mow
His lawn precisely at the point you scream.
I do not know the man. I know the woman:
I left her at a bridge inside a dream,
Since when she has aged terribly. My sin
Is not that you were murdered in my head
As a man in my own shoes stood idly by,
But that I let you lure me into bed
With that same trick I taught you – I, I, I.
Three twitches of the curtain, and I stepped
Into your lamplight while another slept.

7

As the cat eats wax from your ear-finger,
Symphony Orchestra Baden-Baden
Plays the Fifth. You look up. 'No high drama,'
You say, and curl back to your magazine
With that new-wife look certain men would kill for.
You're baffled by my air of absence-presence
(Which, happily, young doctors have a pill for).
Ah, but all's resolved with a major cadence:
I lie with you in many ways. None fails.
The cat's next door now, overturning something.
Downstairs a small girl practises her scales.
'I met the mother. Nice. No wedding ring.'
The days go by, the nights, an even pace.
You confiscate my Luger, just in case.

8

Madeleine, the word is out. Quick, let's go
And find some floor to lie on. Finish dressing
In the car (I'll drive). Oh love, don't be slow.
These rooms aren't safe now. Time is pressing.
And you can always come back by yourself
In a little while.

              Please, don't look at me
Like that. I'm not mad. Nothing's on the shelf
That we can't go without. Don't cry. You'll see,
In a little while, just how hopeless
It always was, our living in this city,
Where everything's permitted, nothing is.
They say the wolf's returning. There's a way
To live condemned with his air of being free
That we can't go without. Don't cry. You'll see.

9

This is the bread of exile, this the cup
With birds and blueberries, your favourite. Not
Austere enough? We can always make it up:
Rub our hands for warmth, drink from a tin pot –
Anything other than sit in this silence
Where shadows lengthen and diminish, and,
Before we're done, the bread basket's a fence,
The butter knife is spreading grains of sand
On slabs of slate. You miss the 'old us'. Yes,
I miss us too: quite nice people, we were.
Forget all that. Don't think of this as less –
It's not been given to us to 'prefer'.
We're in an altered world. A simple dish,
With bread beside, has everything we wish.

It's no life, not for you. I see that now.

Forgive me, love. And when you're done forgiving,

Forgive me still. A child who beat her brow

Against her wall at night knows well reliving

Terror is no life. Not for you. For me,

My part, I thought to take you in my arms,

Take you bodily somewhere you would be,

As the hymnist says, safe from all alarms –

A quiet summerhouse, some dear green place

Where the dragonfly whirrs uneven wings –

Would smooth away the terror from your face,

The terror I utterly can't bear.

                       These things

You've seen I would not wish on any daughter.

Forgive me. I forgot how young you were.

In the studied brown air, old heads are smoking.

'What, pray, is the time value of money?'

The one with fish-eyes asks. He isn't joking,

And I can't tell yet if it's yesterday,

Or last year, or a century ago.

'I lost my love. The Black Rider took her.

Have you seen her? Or him?' The old heads know

On the bang of a gong it's time for supper;

Already their thick jowls salivate.

Menus are called for. A cipher fetches.

'Gentlemen, you are old. I am too late.

You cannot help me.' Old fish-eyes retches:

'The time value of money is the fear

Of losing what you've lost. No girl passed here.'

Here's how I found you, finally: foot in hand

And staring at the wall. 'A speck, a flaw,

The least thing bears most love. You understand?'

I didn't spare your feelings, still so raw.

'I hate all that. Don't want to lose desire.'

Your hurt look, non-serene, was like a kiss.

'Us, here,' I went on, 'that's real. Nothing's higher.'

After our exile, our return, your bliss

Was in another place. I couldn't get there,

However much I made out not to try.

That room you moved round by degrees: we met there,

You in black, with your long straight back, and I

Aghast that I had made you so still.

                                 Race

Towards me, love. I'm staring into space.

A NOTE ON THE AUTHOR

David Cameron is a Glasgow-born poet and novelist. In 2014 he received the Hennessy Literary Award. He is, according to Ron Butlin, 'one of the most insightful and thought-provoking poets around', and his poetry (collected in *The Bright Tethers* and *Korean Letters*) has also been praised by Seamus Heaney and Liz Lochhead, among others. Reviewing Cameron's first collection of fiction, *Rousseau Moon*, Robert Nye wrote that his work 'transmutes the base matter of common experience into something like gold'; Alistair Braidwood described Cameron's experimental novel, *Prendergast's Fall*, as 'one of the most inventive and interesting novels of recent times'. Cameron has also written a critical study, *Samuel Beckett: The Middle and Later Years*. He continues to work closely with the Toronto-based composer David Jaeger on several settings of his poems. From late 2000 to mid-2004, Cameron lived in Amsterdam, where *Femke* is set.

www.davidcameronpoet.com